M000312583

GREAT AND SMALL

IN DOG TOWN

SANDY RIDEOUT

ELLEN RIGGS

n Dog Town

andy Rideout

ights under copyright reserved
eproduced, stored in or introduced
ny form, or by any means without

s, places and incidents are either
d fictitiously. Any resemblance to
lead, is entirely coincidental.

-36-8 eBook
-37-5 Book
C Kindle
Paperback

Rideout
ut.com
u Harper
larke
6

Great and Small

Copyright © 2019

All rights reserved. Without limiting the
above, no part of this publication may be
into a retrieval system, or transmitted, in
the prior written permission of the author

This is a work of fiction. Names, character
products of the author's imagination or use
actual events, locales, or persons, living or

ISBN 978-1-98930
ISBN 978-1-98930
ASIN B07SLT3L
ASIN 1989303374

Publisher: Sandy
www.sandyride
Cover designer: Lo
Editor: Serena
210310205

WELCOME TO DOG TOWN!

Dear Reader,

I used to be a diehard cat lady. Then I got my first dog ever and I was a goner! A journalist by training, I interviewed every expert I could find: trainers, breeders, groomers, walkers and more. The journey ultimately brought me here, to Dog Town.

Dorset Hills, better known as *Dog Town*, is famous for being the most dog-friendly place in the world. People come from near and far to enjoy its beautiful landscape and unique charms. Naturally, when so many dogs and dog-lovers unite in one town, mischief and mayhem ensue.

In the Dog Town cozy-romance series, you can expect the humor, the quirky, loveable characters and the edge-of-your-seat suspense that are part of any cozy mystery, but there's a little more romance and a lot less murder. In fact, *no one dies*! I can guarantee you'll laugh out loud and enjoy hair-raising adventures, heartwarming holidays and happily-ever-afters for both humans and pets.

You can read the books in any order, but it's more fun to work your way through the seasons in Dog Town:

- *Ready or Not in Dog Town* (The Beginning)
- *Bitter and Sweet in Dog Town* (Labor Day)
- *A Match Made in Dog Town* (Thanksgiving)

- *Lost and Found in Dog Town* (Christmas)
- *Calm and Bright in Dog Town* (Christmas)
- *Tried and True in Dog Town* (New Year's)
- *Yours and Mine in Dog Town* (Valentine's Day)
- *Nine Lives in Dog Town* (Easter)
- *Great and Small in Dog Town* (Memorial Day)
- *Bold and Blue in Dog Town* (Independence Day)
- *Better or Worse in Dog Town* (Labor Day)

If you fancy more murder with your mystery, be sure to join my newsletter at **Sandyrideout.com** to get the FREE PREQUEL to the Bought-the-Farm Cozy Mystery series. My newsletter is filled with funny stories and photos of my adorable dogs. Don't miss out!

Take care,
Sandy (and Ellen)

CHAPTER ONE

The curved, wrought iron sign framing the long gravel driveway read, "Runaway Farm." Or at least, it had, before the "m" rusted out and pretty much disintegrated. Dust whirled up on a breeze and sifted over the bushes on either side of the winding lane, giving the place the look of a ghost town in an old western movie. It wasn't at all what you'd expect to see on the outskirts of the small but thriving city of Dorset Hills.

"You're sure this is it, ma'am?" the driver asked, checking the rearview mirror to see if anyone was coming up behind them. This stretch of highway probably didn't see a lot of traffic, being on the wrong side of the region's gorgeous rolling hills. No one really wanted to live this far from either the quaint town or the well-groomed trails.

Hannah Pemberton pulled her eyes away from the sign to stare at the back of the driver's head. Had he really just called her ma'am? She was barely 34 and looked younger, at least according to her esthetician. Quality products, frequent facials and broad-brimmed hats would keep her that way if she had anything to say about it.

The driver turned. "Ma'am?"

There it was again! He obviously wasn't too concerned about getting a good tip.

Peering out again, she said, "Runaway Farm? I doubt it. My friend texted me an address and told me to meet her there." She offered her phone through the seats, and added, "Sir."

The driver, no more than 22, turned, startled. After checking her phone, he said, "Then I guess we're here, Miss Pemberton."

"Miss" wasn't much better than "ma'am," but by this point she should be used to people bumbling around her. It had been six years since she inherited a small fortune—less than people imagined, but more than she'd ever need—from her mother, a successful artist. Before that, she'd just been regular Hannah Pemberton, an overqualified project coordinator for a community agency. Now she was Ma'am and Miss and occasionally got driven around because she'd never learned to drive. There was no point owning a car in New York City. Trains, cabs and her own two feet did the trick.

When she visited her hometown of Dorset Hills, however, getting around was a hassle. This time she'd paid the only limo service in town to ferry her to the outskirts to meet Remi Malone, who'd mentioned an exciting business opportunity. Hannah was looking for a point of re-entry to Dorset Hills. If Remi thought this place was it, she'd get a piece of her mind.

"Let's take a look," she told the driver.

The sedan eased down the driveway, skirting the worst of the bumps and potholes. Letting a property go to seed was unusual for Dorset Hills, even on the fringes. Since the town had been named the best place in North America for dogs and dog-lovers, pressure was extremely high to keep homes and neighborhoods attractive. The owner of Runaway Farm obviously didn't get the memo.

Remi was standing on the porch as the sedan pulled up in front of a dilapidated ranch-style home that was a decade past needing fresh paint and significant repairs. Wide and welcoming at one point, the porch now listed to one side. The eavestrough dangled dangerously at the corner, ready to decapitate someone in a strong wind.

Remi's wave was as jaunty as ever as she skipped over a missing plank and ran down the rickety steps. She pulled Hannah into a hug before she was even out of the car.

"It's so good to see you," Remi said. "You look fantastic."

"I look like an old lady, apparently," Hannah said, glaring back at the car. "It must be the Dog Town air."

"Ridiculous. You could win the Miss Dog Town contest at the spring fair next week." Grinning, Remi added, "That's a compliment."

"If you have to explain it's a compliment, it's not much of one, is it?"

"Oh Hannah, you don't need me to tell you you're gorgeous." Remi shook her head. "Why so touchy today?"

"Just queasy from the ride, I guess." Hannah stared around at the derelict property, wondering if it would look better in sunshine. The skies were gray and heavy with much-needed rain. "Two questions: First, why are we here? And second, where's Leo?"

"First, let me get Leo," Remi said. "He's inside, working."

Remi's beagle, Leo, was a trained therapy dog who'd wrapped half the town around his paw and annoyed the other half with his cheeky opportunism. He was quick with a wag and even quicker to devour whatever fell into his path.

"Should I tell the driver to wait?" Hannah called after Remi, who was taking the stairs two at a time.

"We'll be awhile," Remi said, opening the screen door. "I'll drive you back."

Hannah sent the driver off, and waited for the cloud of dust to settle before taking a good look around. Runaway Farm consisted of a rickety barn, a couple of ramshackle outbuildings, several empty paddocks and green fields beyond. It seemed abandoned, but the stench of manure suggested otherwise. Looking down, Hannah saw that her black suede boots had greyed with dust. The cuffs of her wool pants were coated, too. Remi said she'd scheduled an important meeting, so Hannah had expected a boardroom, not a barn. Mind you, since they'd reconnected last fall, Remi had surprised her with many strange requests, all of them requiring Hannah to open her wallet—her third wallet in eight months, thanks to Leo's taste for fine leather.

In a few minutes, Remi came back with Leo on a leash. The dog's tail started spinning like a propeller when he caught sight of Hannah and he quickly added dusty pawprints to her boots and pants. She stooped to scoop him up. There was no point resisting the most lovable beagle on the planet. Burying her face in his silky fur, she instantly recalled why she was back in Dorset Hills: she needed a dog of her own, a home with room to expand, and a real community. Her wish list was long, but she was patient. There was no rush.

"So, why are we here?" Hannah asked again.

"To meet Bob Hess," Remi said. "The owner. He hasn't been well, but he's ready to see you now."

"Would you mind briefing me on why I'm meeting with Bob Hess of Runaway Farm *before* I barge into his home?"

Remi gave one of her sweet smiles that were almost as hard to resist as Leo. She used that charm for good as a fundraiser for the hospital foundation, and a supporter of canine causes, great and small. Just like Leo, however, if you gave Remi an inch, she took a yard.

"Well..." Remi began tentatively, "the place needs to be sold and Bob wants you to have it."

Hannah gasped, sucking in dust and dog hair. "I am not buying a farm. Are you crazy, Remi Malone? This place is a dump."

"Shut up!" someone with a high-pitched voice screeched through the screen door. "Shut up!"

Hannah covered her mouth in horror. Bob's wife must have heard her call their home a dump. She'd have to send flowers later, with an apology.

"It's not a dump at all," Remi said. "Sure, it could use some polish, but when the sun's shining it's quaint and picturesque. You'll see."

"I won't see," Hannah whispered through her fingers. "Because I'm not staying."

"Go home, lassie," the disembodied voice called. "You stink."

"Rude!" Hannah said, a little louder.

Remi laughed. "You did call the place a dump."

Crossing her arms, Hannah scowled. "Just how big a sucker do you think I am? I can't drive a car let alone a tractor."

Remi dismissed this with a wave. "It's only a hobby farm and you don't have to run the place yourself. There's already a manager. Didn't you tell me you wanted to make a change? To invest in Dorset Hills?"

Hannah's eyebrows rose like nervous crows. "This isn't the kind of investment I had in mind. Not even close. I was thinking of a tea shop, maybe. Or a quaint inn."

"Exactly! This could be a tea shop *and* a quaint inn. Or a bed and breakfast. Use your imagination. People could come from all over to savor the hobby farm experience. There's a horse, some hens, a few sheep and the sweetest pair of heifers."

"Heifers? Well, then you're sidestepping one very obvious cow flap," Hannah said. "I'm the citiest of city girls. I can't even imagine running a farm."

"We'll find you a nice condo with a view of Lake Longmuir and you can call the shots from there. It's no harder than running any business, and of course all of us will be on hand to help."

"All of us?" Hannah squinted suspiciously. "This is Cori Hogan's idea, isn't it? The place needs to be rescued and the town's most illustrious dog rescuer has offered my services."

"She prefers 'notorious,'" Remi said, laughing. "Either way, it was truly Bob's idea. He suggested it when he was in the hospital. Leo and I were on a therapy visit and Bob had just gotten his diagnosis."

Hannah took a step backwards, clutching Leo tighter. "Diagnosis?"

"He's dying," Remi said simply. "He wanted to come home, so Mim Gardiner is nursing him through the last stretch."

"I am not going in there." Hannah backed even further away. "I can't say no to a dying man. And I can't say yes to buying a run-down farm."

Remi came after her but Hannah hurried down the driveway. Leo whined, but he pushed his head under

Hannah's chin. When the going got tough, Leo got serious with his therapeutic measures.

"I know this is tough after what you went through with your mom," Remi said, following her.

"Don't go there, Remi." Stumbling into a pothole, Hannah fought to keep her balance.

"You've told me over and over that you want to make a difference in the world, and here's your chance. You only live once, right?"

Hannah turned and tried to pass Leo to Remi. The dog went limp in her arms, protesting the transfer. "Take him, Remi. I'm going to walk out to the highway and call for a ride."

A cloud of dust came whirling down the driveway after them. Leo gave a low growl and found enough muscle tone to lift his head.

"It's Prima," Remi said, as a fawn-colored terrier mix materialized from the grit. "Cori placed her with Bob last year. He's worked wonders, but she's still a holy terror. Hates everyone except Bob and Cori."

Prima's growl overlapped with Leo's as she circled Hannah's boots, snuffling loudly. Then the little dog threw her head back and gave three sharp barks.

Hannah looked down at the terrier's face. Most dogs were cute, but Prima was decidedly homely. "No one likes a mouthy terrier, Prima."

Tilting her head, Remi said, "I've only seen her do that with Bob. Pick her up."

"So she can savage my face? I won't win Miss Dog Town if that happens."

Laughing, Remi reached for Leo. "I told you, Bob's worked wonders. She's just one of the many homeless animals he's adopted over the years. It's practically bankrupted him, too, and now he's facing leaving them alone. His relatives have made it clear they'll sell this place to the highest bidder. Animal services will come out with a truck."

"Can't he leave the farm in trust to the City?" Hannah asked. "They could turn it into a heritage site, like they did with Dayton Manor and St. Elgin museum."

"Developers are lining up like vultures waiting to swoop in," Remi said. "The property is worth a bomb."

"I'm sure Bill Bradshaw won't let that happen." Hannah stared down at Prima, who stared back with bright button eyes.

Remi snuggled Leo, sighing. "When has Mayor Bradshaw ever backed what's right?"

"I thought he'd embraced a spiritual lifestyle and mellowed."

Turning back to the house, Remi said, "Not so much that he'd miss a chance to help Dog Town grow. Priorities."

Hannah resumed her retreat, but Prima wrapped two paws around her pant leg. Her tawny hind legs dragged behind her, leaving streaks in the gravel. "Prima, I feel for you, girl, but you deserve better than someone like me. I haven't a clue how to rehabilitate a farm."

"Typical terrier," Remi said. "Stubborn. Grabs what she wants and holds on."

Shoving her bag over her shoulder, Hannah stooped to disengage the dog, and then lifted her. There was something about the bristly little scrapper that appealed to her. "What about Bob's wife? She said I stink."

Remi's brow furrowed and then she laughed. "Bob's not married. That was Duncan, the parrot."

"A parrot? You've got to be joking. This is a setup, right? There are cameras around the corner and I'll end up on some lame reality TV show."

"Now there's an idea," Remi said, heading up the front stairs. "For now, let's hurry. Bob tires easily."

"I'm not keeping the place." Hannah tried to set Prima down but she'd learned a thing or two from Leo about passive resistance. "I'll see it through the transition. That's all."

"I'll be right by your side," Remi said, holding the door open. "Now, watch out for the bird. He prefers blondes."

CHAPTER TWO

The thump on the back of Hannah's head sent her staggering forward a couple of feet. "What the—?"

"Duncan, off!" Remi batted the parrot lightly with a piece of cardboard she'd snatched as they entered the house. "He packs quite a wallop for a one-pound bird, doesn't he?"

"Hussy, go home," Duncan squawked, fluttering onto a shelf by the door.

Hannah lifted her bag to cover her head. "That thing could blind me."

"No one's lost an eye," Remi said. "Yet." She wagged a finger at Duncan and nudged Hannah ahead with her other hand. "Be nice, Duncan. This could be your new owner, if you play your cards right."

"What a mess," Duncan croaked. "What a mess."

"I'd have to agree with him," Hannah whispered. "What have you gotten me into, Remi Malone?"

"It's the opportunity of a lifetime." Remi's smile lit up the dim living room. "Sometimes those come in strange packages."

Hannah looked around at the dated furniture and dark

panelling and shook her head. This certainly wasn't her dream come true. She'd imagined herself in a charming century home in Dorset Hills, with wainscoting, plate rails, and the scent of cinnamon in the air. This place smelled of bird poop, dog hair and old kitty litter. The legs of the couch and even the baseboards had been chewed. A layer of dust on the coffee table was etched with what appeared to be claw and wing prints.

"It looks lived-in, doesn't it?" someone asked.

Hannah turned to see a tall, very thin man standing in the doorway. His smile was warm, but his eyes seemed full of a weary sadness. It reminded her of her mother in those terrible last weeks. Her throat tightened as the old sorrow washed over her body like a damp, heavy fog. She hadn't realized that the fog of grief had mostly gone until it came back.

"I guess it does look lived-in," she said, forcing a smile as Remi made the introductions.

Bob walked over to the recliner and sat down, motioning for Remi and Hannah to take the couch opposite. Prima parked herself beside Bob's chair, with her ears pricked.

"That's because it was," he said. "I lived the heck out of this house. If the walls could talk, they'd..."

Duncan screeched an obscenity from the front hall, cutting Bob off.

Hannah and Remi both laughed, but Bob shook his head. "That bird. He's not stupid, you know. I've taught him at least 50 words since I rescued him 10 years ago, but he prefers what he learned before coming."

"Gets a better reaction," Hannah suggested.

"Exactly. Now you're thinking like a parrot," Bob said.

"Thanks. I think." She put her bag down and brushed

as much pet hair from her pants as she could. It seemed to have woven into the fabric already.

"Waste of time," Bob said. "If you're going to take over, you might as well make your peace with fur and feathers."

"I—I can't do that," Hannah said, avoiding Bob's eyes.

"Take over, or make your peace with the mess?" He pushed the recliner back with a thump. Other than his gauntness and pallor, he looked deceptively alert and healthy.

"Either," she said, picking her bag up again. "Remi told me you'd like me to buy Runaway Farm, and—"

"I never said 'buy,'" Bob interrupted. "I said, 'take over.' I don't want your money."

Hannah blinked a few times. Since she'd inherited her mother's estate, it seemed like *everyone* wanted her money. She had learned to come into every conversation with her guard up. Many of the stories she heard were terribly sad, but the causes often didn't align with her mother's interests. Although Mavis Pemberton hadn't been prescriptive about how she wanted her estate to be handled, she'd trusted Hannah to make good decisions. She'd never prepared her for how hard it was to say no.

"Why would you give me your farm?" Hannah glanced at Remi, who looked equally baffled. "I mean, of all people, I'm the least likely to run a farm."

Bob shrugged. "That's what you think. I have a different opinion."

Duncan hopped from chair to chair until he landed on the back of Bob's recliner. The bird was mostly grey, with white patches on his face, and brilliant red tailfeathers. Staring at Hannah with yellow eyes, he croaked, "Hussy."

"That's *not* my opinion," Bob said, laughing. "Duncan speaks for himself."

Hannah tried again. "Why would you think the farm you love should go to a complete stranger?"

"You're not a complete stranger," he said. "I grew up with your mother, and knew her well."

Hannah fumbled with her bag and almost dropped it. The commotion startled Duncan, who hopped along the arm of Bob's chair to keep a closer eye on her.

"You kept in touch?" Doubt and hope blended in her voice in equal measure.

Bob nodded. "Up until she got sick. I guess she didn't want me to know about that. Now I understand how she felt."

"She never mentioned you," Hannah said, plucking tawny hairs from her sleeve. She had to be cautious. Many had falsely claimed to know Mavis in an effort to get to know her money.

"May and I went to school together," Bob said. "Used to walk our dogs in the hills, back before this town got silly. She had Prudence, then, her first wolfhound. And Sarge, a brindle dachshund with a temper. Bit me a few times when I got too friendly."

Hannah stared at him for a moment. "Are you saying you dated my mother?"

It wasn't that hard to believe Bob had been handsome once. He still had a head of salt and pepper hair, and his eyes were startlingly blue. But he couldn't be more different than her conservative father. On the other hand, her parents had had a bumpy marriage and a friendly divorce.

"More like courted," Bob said. "I didn't even have a car, then, so I just hung around hoping. I proposed, but she broke my heart and married your dad and his red Mustang."

Hannah's gasp startled Leo, who left Remi's feet to sit beside Hannah's. Prima gave a warning growl, which Leo returned half-heartedly. Duncan piped up again with, "What a mess."

"You proposed to my mom?"

"Three times, if you must know." Bob laughed a little. "Didn't blame her for saying no, to be honest. Your dad was going places. I was still finding myself." He fidgeted in his chair as if trying to find a comfortable position. "Took another decade."

"I... I don't know what to say," Hannah murmured, turning to Remi. "This is all quite a surprise."

"It's news to me," Remi said, leaning over to pull Leo back. She lifted him into her lap and hugged him, a sure sign she was anxious.

"And you stayed in touch with my mom. After my parents married?"

"Not right away," Bob said. "I left town for a long time. Worked my way around hill country before I finally came home and bought this place. I wouldn't have disrespected your dad by reaching out first. Your mom called me eventually, and we talked now and then."

It seemed like all the dust had lodged in Hannah's throat. She tried to speak and nothing came out but a dry rasp. "Oh."

Bob pushed the chair upright, dislodging Duncan, who fluttered to the coffee table and made more pretty dust angels. "It's not what you're thinking. We were just friends, and barely that. Your dad was a respectable businessman and I was up to my armpits in rescue work. I wasn't always on the right side of the law, although I was always on the right side of animals. I didn't want your mom to know about that."

"Did she find out?" Hannah asked.

"Hard to say. All I know is that I had a secret benefactor

for a long time. Someone literally kept the place afloat with monthly donations. And whenever something big went down—like the time I brought home 16 abused St. Bernards —extra money arrived. Somehow it was always enough to get things sorted out. Even the pair of llamas someone dumped here got the royal treatment, thanks to this private donor. Mostly I found good homes for the rescues, and those that couldn't be placed, stayed with me. No animal in need ever got turned away, and I thank your mother for that."

"Why do you think it was her? I mean, if your benefactor was anonymous?"

He shrugged again. "Because the donations stopped six years ago, when she passed." He let that sink in for a moment. "After that, I ran into money trouble for the first time. My heart had gotten used to saying yes to every sad case. Now my wallet had to say no. The last few years have been really hard."

Bob struggled to push the chair back again. Remi rose to help, shoving Leo into Hannah's arms.

"You're running out of steam," Remi told Bob.

"I'm running out of time," he said, looking at Hannah. "I left some statements on the kitchen table. See if I'm right about your mom." Then he raised his eyes to the ceiling. "Don't tell me if I'm wrong. I like remembering it this way."

Hannah's mind fluttered like the parrot on the dusty table. "Tilly and Randall," she said, at last.

Bob smiled instantly. "She told you about the llamas?"

"Tilly was white, Randall was brown and their baby, Piccata, was a mix. Mom said the baby was the cutest thing she ever saw."

"Well, she never told me she came by. I'm glad she got to see the results of her kindness."

Remi cleared her throat. "I guess that explains the llama trio in your mom's watercolors."

"I'd love to see those," Bob said, although all the energy had drained from his voice. "Another day."

Hannah slid forward on the couch and set Leo on the floor. "You can't give me your farm, Bob. Even if my mom did help finance it."

"I can do whatever I want with my land," he said. "Besides, it's practically yours already. Well, yours and your brother's."

She shook her head. "I can't take it. I wouldn't have the first clue, and James wouldn't, either."

"You'll figure it out. Your mom was a smart lady. Even if she did turn me down." He managed a grin. "Just do the right thing for the animals. I trust you."

"Don't trust me with that. It's too much." Her voice was sharp enough to startle Duncan, who rose up awkwardly and flew at her head again, uttering shrill curses.

Bob snapped his fingers, and Duncan flew over to settle on his arm. "You'll want to wear a hat till he gets used to you."

"Bob, I'm not letting you give me Runaway Farm. End of story."

"Fine, then. Buy it." He glared at her. "I'll donate the money to rescue causes. My nephews won't get a cent of it. They're in cahoots with that idiot."

"Mayor Bradshaw," Remi explained to Hannah. "Like I said earlier, he wants to develop the land."

Bob leaned back and closed his eyes. "At least your mother didn't marry him."

"Bill Bradshaw? Are you saying—"

"I'm tired." Bob interrupted. "Just promise me you'll

keep my farm safe, or I'll send Duncan after you again. He really prefers—"

"Blondes," Hannah said. "I know. Well, I'm not dyeing my hair for that bird. That's going above and beyond."

"You'll have your hands full without hair appointments." Bob flicked his fingers toward the door without opening his eyes. "Just promise me."

"Okay," Hannah said. "I promise. But can't we at least talk about other solutions?"

"Like I said, I trust you. And so does Prima." Bob gestured to her feet, and she saw the terrier had crept over at some point to lie beside her. "Maybe you'll even teach this parrot some manners. He's smarter than the mayor, you know."

Hannah and Remi laughed as they got up, and then squealed as Duncan chased them to the door. Prima came after them, too, snapping at Remi's heels.

"What a circus," Hannah said, as they stood on the porch. She stared around at the farm again, this time her eyes full of tears.

Remi hugged her, with Leo squished in between them. "It's going to be fine. Maybe even fun."

"I never liked the circus," Hannah grumbled, as Remi led her down the stairs. "Dorset Hills is crazy."

"It grows on you," Remi said. "Or you get crazy, too."

CHAPTER THREE

A woman in denim overalls squeezed Hannah's hand so hard her knees almost buckled and then said, "Pleasure to meet you, Mrs. Pemberton."

The woman's eyebrows came together in a ruddy streak as she scanned Hannah from head to foot. Although she'd worn jeans, flat boots, a ponytail and minimal makeup for her first official visit, Hannah sensed she was already failing as Bob's successor in the eyes of Fox Spinner, Runaway Farm's current manager.

"You too," Hannah said, not bothering to correct the title. "Bob spoke so highly of you. He said the farm couldn't be in better hands."

"I'm sure he meant yours, not mine," Fox said. "You do own the place."

The nickname apparently came from Fox's deep red hair, since she wasn't particularly foxy. Her eyes were small and dark, and her skin was the deep bronze of someone who never worried about sunscreen. She hadn't mustered a smile, but Hannah cut her some slack. The farm manager was probably grieving her loss. Bob had passed only a few days after signing over the farm. It had felt awkward and sad, but at their last meeting, he'd squeezed Hannah's hands and thanked her. She hoped that meant she'd done the right thing. If her mother had been the secret donor, she'd hidden her tracks well. Even so, Hannah suspected it was true. So many odd farm animals had found their way into her mom's art. Now it seemed like a secret code.

Turning to a stall that held a tall dark horse with a gray muzzle, Hannah said, "I'm paying the bills, but you're the heart of the place. Bob was clear about that, and Cori Hogan agrees. You know how hard she is to please."

She turned back in time to see the first flicker of light on Fox's face. Cori Hogan, the best dog trainer in Dorset Hills, was generally either revered or reviled. Fox was apparently in the former camp. Hannah admired Cori's spirited defence of all things canine, but her compassion didn't extend to all things human. Many people fell short in Cori's eyes, and Hannah was one of them. Being wealthy was evidently a sign of poor character, no matter how generously Hannah gave to animal causes.

"I'd show you around," Fox said, straightening her shoulders. "But you'd ruin your boots."

"Let's do it," Hannah said. "I'm excited to meet the crew."

Fox turned and led Hannah out the double rear doors of the mid-sized barn. It had been a working farm long ago, but most of the stalls were empty now.

"Our numbers are down," Fox said. "Bob pulled in a lot of favors to get animals placed after he got sick." Her eyelashes fluttered, as she fought tears. "We lost the sweetest pair of goats. Total characters. I bottle fed them from birth after their mom died. And Eeyore... I never thought anyone would claim that donkey. He was such a grump."

"Who'd take a cranky donkey?" Hannah asked, picking her way through cow and horse manure to the paddocks.

"Sheep farmer," Fox said. "Donkeys make good guardians. They'll kick a coyote to death protecting their flocks."

"Killer donkeys? I guess I have a lot to learn."

Fox gave her the cut-eye. "Ya think?"

A flicker of fire warmed Hannah's belly. She hadn't expected a hero's welcome, given the circumstances, but she'd hoped Fox would respect Bob's wishes. Surely the woman realized this was the last place Hannah would choose to be. Why not give her the benefit of the doubt?

"I think I'm a pretty quick study. And I certainly know when I need to rely on expert help." Forcing a smile, Hannah added, "Is there any way we could get your goats back?"

Fox's expression softened immediately but she shook her head. "They're settled now. Besides, another animal in need always comes along."

Hannah supressed a shudder. She wasn't looking to expand, only maintain for Bob's sake. In fact, if she could, she'd rehome the remaining animals, starting with Duncan, the belligerent parrot. Every time she went into the house he ambushed her. There was a gash in the back of her neck where he'd pecked her after screeching either "stupid lassie" or "slutty hussy." With the bird's Scottish brogue, it was hard to know. One of his previous owners had been no gentleman.

A quick tour introduced her to the two heifers, one black-and-white, the other brown-and-white, a quartet of fluffy white sheep, and a large flock of chickens in a huge, wired-over pen. As a child, Hannah had visited agricultural fairs on school trips, but it seemed like there were more types of hens now. Wasn't one egg pretty much the same as another?

A rooster with bronze feathers strutted over and tilted his head to stare up at her with one eye.

"That's Aladdin," Fox said. "He keeps the harem happy and laying. There are more eggs every day than we can handle. Bob used to deliver them to the seniors in the neighborhood." She gave Hannah a pointed look. "Maybe your driver could carry on the tradition."

A flush rose around Hannah's collar and she zipped her jacket to conceal it. It was hard enough for newcomers to fit in around Dog Town. The driver made it impossible.

"I think I hear a car now," Hannah said, grateful to change the subject. "Have I met everyone?"

"Yeah. It's just the horse, cows, sheep and the chickens," Fox said. "For now."

"Plus Prima and Duncan," Hannah added.

"They're house pets. That's different."

Judging by her tan, baggy overalls and smirk, Fox didn't like being confined by clothing, walls or common courtesy. But if Hannah kept trying, maybe they could find a point of connection.

A horn blared and they walked around the perimeter of the barn. Six vehicles had lined up in the large parking area in front of the house. Hannah recognized Bridget Linsmore's lime-green van, Cori Hogan's battered pickup truck, Remi's beater sedan, Arianna Torrance's white SUV, and a gray government-owned Prius that Kinney Butterfield normally drove. At the end of the line was a shiny cherry-red pickup she didn't recognize. Doors seemed to open all at once, spilling well over a dozen people onto the driveway.

Almost everyone Hannah knew in Dorset Hills rushed over, and swallowed her up into hug after hug.

Finally someone gave her breathing room and stuck out a gloved hand with a neon-orange middle finger. Hannah smiled as she squeezed the glove with her right hand. Cori Hogan's handshake had always been assertive, but Fox's grip made the petite trainer seem like a shrinking violet.

"Good to see you, Cori," Hannah said, smiling.

Cori ran her gloved hand over short dark hair as sleek and dark as a mink's, and left it flyaway. "I know. It's like a royal visit, right?"

Hannah was the first to laugh but many joined her. Cori's arrogance was legendary and only partly tongue-in-cheek.

"I wish I had something worthy to offer you," Hannah said. "But the cupboards are practically bare."

Buttoning her denim jacket against a brisk May breeze, Cori shrugged. "No worries. I have plenty to offer you. Advice, mainly. Consider it a housewarming gift."

"You mean 'farmwarming,'" Remi said, taking up a position at Hannah's side. She'd made a promise to stand by her and evidently meant to keep it.

"Because Cori's such a farm expert." The voice came from a woman with a sweet face and dark hair falling past her shoulders. "When's the last time you milked a cow?"

"The same day you did, I guess," Cori said. "Or did they tutor you on that in dog cop school?"

Kinney Butterfield just grinned. "All we learned in dog cop school is to stay a step ahead of troublemakers. In fact, there's a whole segment on the pet Rescue Mafia, complete with a really old photograph of you."

Cori held up her orange middle finger. "Take a new one."

Slinging Leo under one arm, Remi nudged in between the two women. "Play nice, ladies. It's a housewarming party."

"A party?" Hannah said. "I'm not even going to live in the house, and like I said, there's no food."

"Oh, there's food," Remi said, raising her free arm. "Hit it, people."

The crowd dispersed to open doors and trunks and hatches. Coolers, baskets and clattering china appeared. There was enough food to feed an army. The thought made Hannah smile. In many ways, they were an army of like-minded people drawn together by an extreme love of dogs, and an equally extreme loathing for the current city council. Cori might step up as ringleader in tough times, but Remi was often the lynchpin who held strong personalities together.

Bridget Linsmore and her tall, black dog, Beau, led the way to the house, followed by Maisie Todd, Nika Lothian, and Andrea MacDuff, the other formal members of the Rescue Mafia. These women could skillfully extract a dog from desperate circumstances, but were just as capable of staging an impromptu community fete. Hannah had never met so many bright, talented and quirky people in New York, nor in her travels around the world. Her shoulders relaxed and her breathing evened out as they surrounded her and carried her along.

"It'll be fine," Remi said, trying to pass over Leo.

Hannah crossed her arms and refused delivery. "Prima gets jealous. I left her inside because Fox said she scares the chickens."

"And Fox scares everyone," Remi muttered.

"Except me," Cori said. Being slight and fleet of foot, she managed to infiltrate private conversations easily. "Fox

Spinner has a good head and a heart for animals, even if she's not as polished as I am."

Remi laughed. "No one's as polished as you are."

"Or as smart. Luckily." She looked up at Hannah. "We'll have to stay on our toes around here, Hannah. I heard the mayor's gunning for you."

"Gunning for me? Why? He's always liked me."

"You mean he's always liked your money," Cori said. "You're worth a lot to him, but this land is apparently worth more. Sullivan Shaw told Bridget that developers were fuming when Bob sold you the land."

"Bob was clear that he didn't want Runaway Farm plowed under and replaced by concrete towers," Remi said.

"I'm a witness to that," said Mim Gardiner. She had a kind face but looked perpetually weary, as if she'd seen too much sadness. That was probably true of most nurses. "As were dozens of others."

"A man can do what he wants with his own land, can't he?" asked Arianna Torrance, Mim's best friend and a popular dog breeder of goldendoodle hybrids. Her long blonde waves would no doubt be a hit with Duncan the parrot.

Bridget fell back and they caught up on the porch. "Sullivan just mentioned the mayor's upset. He's been upset about a lot of things lately."

"As if I didn't have enough to worry about," Hannah said. "I don't even know how to run a farm."

"Don't worry about the mayor," Bridget said. "All I do is breathe and it annoys him. This will die down soon enough."

"And leave the farming to Fox," Cori said. "She's got your back."

"I doubt that," Hannah said. "She's already made a dig about my driver."

Cori smirked. "Can you blame her? I mean, who doesn't know how to drive? It's a rite of passage."

"Not in New York City," Hannah said. "We have other rites there."

"I'll teach you to drive," a deep voice offered. She turned to see a tall, handsome man with dark auburn hair and a ready smile. "We'll have you roadworthy in no time."

Hannah started to smile at the sight of Nick Springdale, but stopped it at half mast. They'd met during her visit at Easter and she suspected he had a bit of a crush on her. There was no point in leading him on. She wasn't crush material.

"Thanks, Nick," she said. "But I'll spare you. That truck looks brand new."

"Rich girls can drive, too," Cori said. "In fact, people would respect you more if you drove a truck. It's a universal law."

Hannah glared at Cori. "If they don't already respect me—"

"They don't," Cori interrupted, grinning.

"Then I'll have to earn it another way."

Nick's brow furrowed and he took a step back. "Is this one of those 'mean girl' situations? My sister told me that happens but she's not here to translate."

"How is Evie?" Hannah asked, happy to change the subject. "I still can't believe how she exposed that exotic pet ring at Easter. She's a hero."

"Still paying for it with a concussion, unfortunately," Nick said, nudging Cori aside so gradually and gently that the tiny trainer either didn't notice or didn't resist. "Jon took her home to our folks for a month to make sure she'd stay out of trouble."

"What about Roberto?" Hannah asked. "That was the most interesting cat I've ever met."

"If you think so, I'll bring him out here," Nick said. "She left Roberto with me and he hasn't stopped pining."

"Cats don't pine," Cori said, trying to shoulder her way back into the conversation.

"This one does." Nick held his ground. "He could hang out in the barn while I give you driving lessons."

Hannah was thinking about how to let him down gently when a small vehicle careened down the driveway and skidded to a dusty stop behind Nick's new truck. "Now *that* car is more my speed," she said.

A woman with salt-and-pepper hair hanging in a long braid jumped out of a golf cart and headed directly for Hannah with her hand outstretched. "Sally Taylor," she said. "Your next-door neighbor. I'm just a mile down the road."

"So lovely to meet you," Hannah said. "Did you know Bob well?"

"Very. And the entire menagerie. I come often to get my pet fix. Sometimes I take over and give Fox a day off."

Hannah looked around, but Fox had apparently gone back to the barn.

"Sally, please join the housewarming party," Hannah said. By now, music was spilling out of the house. When the screen door opened, a small shape dashed out, wove through legs like a seasoned agility dog, and catapulted right into Hannah's arms. "Hey, Prima. So nice of you to wait for an invitation."

Cori snapped her fingers and pointed at the rotting wood at their feet. "Four on the floor. Start with a dog how you mean to go on, Hannah. And don't even get me going about the parrot."

"Oh, Duncan," Sally said, laughing. "That feathered charmer calls me a witch."

"I get 'hussy' a lot," Hannah said. "He keeps telling me to go home."

Nick held the door so they could all pass through. "Teach him some new words," he said. "This is home."

Hannah's eyes darted quickly around the property before she stepped inside. It wasn't home and would never be. She couldn't run away from Runaway Farm fast enough.

Just then a bellow rose above the noise of the crowd. "Incoming," Fox called. "Sheep on the loose."

The crowd shifted into reverse and moved down the stairs toward the barn, with Cori in the lead.

Hannah followed, still holding the terrier. "Prima," she whispered into the dog's scruffy fur. "Wake me when the nightmare's over."

CHAPTER FOUR

Hannah stopped at the top of the wide, worn steps of Dorset Hills City Hall to smooth her hair and check her jacket for dog fur. One day at Runaway Farm had left her frazzled and bedraggled. A long bath and a blowout at the hotel's hair salon hadn't helped as much as she'd hoped. Ever since she'd arrived in Dog Town she'd felt exhausted and queasy and unkempt.

Turning, she stared at the huge bronze German shepherd that sat in the center of Bellington Square below. It was probably the most famous of the dozens of dog statues now dotting the city, and it was certainly the most fearsome. The twin wolfhounds the mayor had purchased for the Barton Gallery of Art with a donation from her mother's estate were alarming—and completely at odds with her artist mom's whimsical aesthetic—but they were sweet pups in comparison to this official city mascot.

Today, it felt like there was a real wolf at her heels, not just a bronze one. The sooner she could sort out the problem of Runaway Farm and get on with her new life, the better. She couldn't in good conscience sell the property, because of her promise to Bob to keep the farm safe. What she *could* do was donate the farm to the right cause, with a ton of legal conditions that kept the spirit of her agreement intact. The City was the most likely contender, but only if it could prove itself worthy of the honor. There would need to be a board of trustees, with membership that included herself and Mafia members. That way, the mayor couldn't wreck it.

Normally Mayor Bradshaw waited for her in the reception area, eager to begin the political wooing without a moment's delay. For nearly nine months, he'd been trying to convince her to move back to Dorset Hills and start some kind of business. He had a new idea every visit: a restaurant, a retail chain catering to pets, an art school, and so on. Nothing had pressed the right buttons. As much as she'd wanted to come home, it had to happen on her terms, not the mayor's. When she settled here, it would be for the long haul. For now, she was only leasing out her New York apartment. No bridges had been burned for this farm rescue.

"Hannah Pemberton," she told the receptionist, who reluctantly pulled out one earbud. "The mayor's expecting me."

Picking up the phone, the young woman said, "Hannah Pemberton to see you, sir. Pemberton. That's right. Hannah Pemberton. She says she has an appointment."

Hannah's eyes narrowed. "He requested the meeting."

The receptionist held an index finger to fuchsia lips. "Yes, sir. I'll tell her, sir." Hanging up, she said, "The mayor's running a bit behind. He'll see you in 20 minutes. There's a cafeteria downstairs if you need coffee."

"I'll wait right here." Hannah perched on the edge of a leather chair in the reception area. After a few minutes, she phoned Remi. "Hey, are you free today?" She raised her voice deliberately. "Let's see if Duff can show us some properties. I'm in the market for a house overlooking Lake Longmuir. A nice big one."

There was a sudden movement and the mayor appeared beside her. "Why hello, Hannah. Come right in. Please."

"Gotta go, Rems," Hannah said, dropping the phone into her purse. She stood up and smiled. "I'm sorry to interrupt, sir. Would you like to rebook?"

"Not at all, don't be silly." The tall, silver-haired man beckoned, and then fell in behind her. As always, his movements were economical and elegant. "I was just taking a moment to gather myself for the day. Leading this city is harder than I make it look."

"I'm sure it is," Hannah said. "There's always something going on around here."

He ushered her into his office and gestured to a guest chair set up in front of his big oak desk. Then he sat down behind the desk in a seat that resembled a throne. "Tell me about your interest in real estate. I'm delighted you're thinking of becoming a homeowner in Dorset Hills."

"I'm already a homeowner in Dorset Hills," she said. "Perhaps you haven't heard that Bob Hess sold me his farm. I took possession yesterday."

The mayor rested his elbows on the desk and steepled his fingertips. "I couldn't quite believe it. What would a woman like you want with that old farm?"

"A woman like me? What kind of woman is that?" Hannah set manicured fingertips on his desk and then regretted it. One nail was jagged and torn after the incident with the sheep the day before. The beast had charged directly at her and she'd climbed a small tree, much to Cori's amusement. *That* was the kind of woman she was— the type that ran when a sheep got testy. On the bright side, she hadn't realized she was so nimble. All those yoga classes weren't a waste.

"A refined woman," the mayor said. "Sophisticated. Cultured." He looked down at her broken nail. "Polished. We need people like you in Dorset Hills."

"Well, I'm happy to be a taxpayer now," she said, smiling. "Although the farm is almost off the Dog Town grid. It's clinging to the county line."

"It's still very much a part of this fine city." Leaning back in his chair, he added, "I would have expected you to live downtown, near all our amenities." Clearing his throat, he added, "And your—uh—friends."

"I would love to be closer to the core, no question. Luckily my friends are happy to visit the farm. They're animal lovers, as you may know."

"We all are. But if you're looking for a new property downtown, perhaps you've decided farm life isn't for you."

That was exactly what she'd decided, but his odd behavior today had unnerved her. No way was she going to offer the farm to him now. She'd have to figure out a plan B.

"I like having the best of both worlds, and Dorset Hills can offer it," she said. "I'll enjoy the restaurants, shops and galleries when I'm downtown and then retreat to the suburbs. It's practically rural."

"Let me help you find the perfect place downtown," he said. "I know some properties that aren't even listed yet. And then I can help you get the best offer for the farm when you're ready to part with it."

"I have no plans at present to part with it, Mayor."

He leaned forward and pinned her with a dark gaze. "Hannah, really. There's no place for a farm in today's Dog Town. That belongs to a bygone era. The only horses in city limits are with the mounted police, and there are no other cattle." He shook his head and his silver hair caught the light. "I've never been comfortable around cows," he said. "They're inherently untrustworthy."

Hannah laughed. "Inherently untrustworthy?"

"Who knows what they're thinking? They play stupid. At least with a dog you always know where you stand."

"I never really gave much thought to cows, sir. Or sheep for that matter. I will say that goats intrigue me."

He leaned back and crossed his arms. "I'd find a new hobby, Hannah. The city's reviewing its zoning guidelines and it's quite likely that all livestock will be formally prohibited in Dorset Hills. Even chickens are banned, you know."

"Lots of people have backyard coops from what I hear," Hannah said. "Bob delivered to all the local seniors. He was so well-loved."

The mayor raised one eyebrow. "Not by his family, I'm afraid. I understand that his nephews are contesting the sale of his land. They say he was not of sound mind when he made the deal. Having met with Bob myself last week, I'd have to agree."

Hannah slid to the edge of her seat and stared at him. "You visited Bob Hess?"

"A few times, yes. I had my doubts about his care. A mayor worries."

"Mim Gardiner was there till late every single night. That means you must have dropped by after 11."

He shrugged, unfazed. "Or on my way to work. I'm an early riser."

"Sir. Please tell me you weren't harassing a dying man about his property."

"Oh, Hannah. Around here we call visits like that being neighborly. In a small community, good leaders go above and beyond for their people."

Flinging herself back, Hannah shook her head. "Poor Bob. I'm so glad he had time to take care of his affairs as he wished."

"His nephews may have a case, I'm afraid. It might be best not to get too entrenched."

"I'm confident my lawyers and Bob's lawyers crossed every T." Nonetheless a seed of doubt planted itself in her mind. While she was confident in her legal team, she knew the mayor was skilled at finding loopholes. "Bob's wishes were well-known. And as I said, he was well-loved."

The mayor got to his feet. "Scratch below the surface and everyone has detractors. Even me."

"I suppose." Taking the hint, Hannah rose herself. "All I can do is honor the commitment I made to him as best I can."

"Let me give you some advice for a peaceful life, Hannah." He walked her to the door with a hand under her elbow. "What you resist persists, and what you embrace dissolves. You really can't go wrong if you keep that in mind."

His hand felt like a claw and she scooted ahead. "I will keep that in mind, Mayor."

"Are you sure you don't want my help to find a nice house that actually suits you?"

She shook her head. "I'm in good hands, thank you."

"A last word, then: leave roughing it to the roughnecks. Come back and let's discuss how we can work together to help this fine city grow."

Giving him what she hoped was a billion-dollar smile, she said, "It's good to be home, sir."

He opened his office door and stepped aside to let her pass. "This city is like a big ol' hug, isn't it?"

A big old hug that could crush you if you weren't careful.

FOLLOWING Duff and Remi up the front steps of a taste-fully restored mansion, Hannah shuddered. "Can you believe him? Harassing a dying man and threatening me like that? I've called my lawyer."

"His bark is worse than his bite," Remi said, as they walked into the marble-floored foyer. "Usually."

"Oh, he bites," said Andrea MacDuff, better known as Duff. As usual, she was impeccable, with sleek auburn hair falling to her shoulders, and an outfit befitting one of the best real estate agents in Dorset Hills. She ran her hand along the white wainscoting and checked her fingers for dust before nodding at no one in particular.

"We find a way around him," Remi said, trailing after Duff into a spacious kitchen that had been recently reno-vated. It smelled of fresh paint and wood shavings.

"Not always," Hannah replied.

"Overall we're winning," Remi said. "I believe good always prevails."

Hannah smiled at her friend. "You have such faith in people. That's why everyone likes you."

"Leo's the one with the pull," Remi said. She turned to give Duff a reproachful glance. "He wasn't welcome today, unfortunately."

"I've banned all dogs from showings," Duff said. "I was always cleaning up hair, pawprints and accidents, so I made it a policy."

"Leo's above any policy," Remi said.

Duff rolled her eyes. "He's got a longer rap sheet than many criminals."

"Now you sound like Cori," Remi said.

"What a terrible thing to say." Duff clicked across the kitchen on high heels, and used her sleeve to rub away invisible spots from an elegant, swooping faucet.

"Ladies." Hannah tapped the granite counter. "Can we focus on my problem with the mayor?"

Duff turned back. "Sure. But maybe we should leave viewings for another day. You've barely looked at any of the homes we've visited."

"I'm sorry." Hannah traced a pattern in the countertop with one finger. "This place is absolutely stunning. But it feels like a museum. Or an art gallery."

Duff pulled out her phone and typed notes into it. "Not homey enough? You're looking for something with a more rustic flavor."

"Like the rustic farm she already owns, maybe," Remi said, grinning. "You're getting attached, aren't you, Hannah?"

"I refuse to get attached to Runaway Farm," Hannah said. "But I do want to honor Bob's legacy."

Duff came over and faced Hannah across the counter. "How about we continue this conversation over lunch? You're not ready to buy, Hannah."

"I'm just a bit rattled. Bob was a kind man and contributed so much to this town, yet the mayor's practically dancing on his grave. I'm not sure I want to live under his rule."

"There's more to this town than Bill Bradshaw," Duff said. "You'd have to go far to find a community like this. In fact, the mayor's mischief has made us stronger."

"I agree," Remi said. "There was never this kind of

community spirit when we were growing up, Hannah. That's why you wanted to meet a nice guy here and settle down to raise a family."

"I believe I said I wanted to meet a nice dog and settle down." Hannah had been careful not to spill too much about her hopes, even to Remi. "And Prima wasn't exactly what I had in mind. I'm waiting for Arianna to breed me the sweet doodle of my dreams."

Remi beckoned and they followed her out of the kitchen and into the grand foyer. "This town will give you exactly what you need, if you just stay open to it."

Walking down the front stairs, Hannah looked over her shoulder. "I need a testy terrier and a provocative parrot?"

"Just give the farm a chance," Remi said.

Hannah straightened her shoulders. "Well, I'm not letting Bill Bradshaw drive me out, that's for sure. My mother always said you can't trust a man who can't trust a cow."

"She did? Really?" Remi asked.

"Not in so many words," Hannah said, grinning. "But Mavis Pemberton didn't suffer fools gladly."

Staring around, her smile faded. Her mom would have hated this street and these mansions. And, as odd as it seemed, she'd apparently loved Runaway Farm.

CHAPTER FIVE

Fox Spinner had come and gone before Hannah got to the farm the next morning. There was a sheet of paper sticking out of the screen door. On one side, it advertised a lawn care service. On the other, in neat capital letters, Fox had written: "I resign, effective immediately." And then, "P.S. The part-timers quit, too."

Pulling out her phone, Hannah called Remi. "Fox quit. No call, no notice. Just a note in the door."

Remi cursed quietly and the profanity carried more weight for being so rare. "I'm sorry to hear that," she said. "Fox scared the crap out of me, but she was good to the animals."

Hannah turned to survey the property and gather her courage. The minute she went into the house she'd be attacked by Duncan the parrot. She had to wear a hat or he'd land on the crown of her head and yank out her hair. Bob had never caged the bird and for the most part, Duncan stuck around his perch in the corner of the living room. For Hannah, however, he boldly hopped and flapped from room to room, waiting for his moment to strike.

"I'll need to find someone else with livestock experience immediately," she told Remi. "Fox had promised to spend the next few days training me on care and feeding. I wanted to make sure I could handle everything in a pinch. She'd worked seven days a week through Bob's illness. Maybe she was just exhausted."

"Let's call a 911," Remi said.

"The police? It's just a farming emergency."

Remi's laugh sounded hollow. "I think it's actually a political emergency. I'm guessing the mayor got to Fox."

"Really?" Hannah took off her hat and waved it at the flies that always seemed to be swarming around. "I thought you liked to see the good in everyone."

"Look at the timing. You met with the mayor yesterday, and now she's quit. And she took the part-timers with her. Let me check in with Bridget and Cori and I'll get back to you."

"I hate to bother them," Hannah said, opening the door slowly. "I can't call on the Mafia every time I need help."

"That's what 'community' means, my friend."

"Well, the way things are going I'll wear out my welcome pretty fast." Peeking around the door, she looked for the telltale flash of the dive-bomber's red tailfeathers. "I've got to become independent here."

There was a pause at the other end. "Cori texted back. They're picking me up and we're coming over." Hannah tried to protest, and Remi spoke over her. "Remember when I said we had your back? This is what it looks like."

Hanging up, Hannah edged into the front hallway. Prima circled her legs in a frenzy of greeting, and actually waited for an invitation into Hannah's arms. Dropping her purse on the floor, she scooped up the wriggling terrier and let the dog lick her chin. It felt strangely validating to be the only person Prima really liked, other than Bob. Without Fox, however, Prima couldn't stay here overnight anymore. Hopefully she could contain her scrappy personality at the Larkson Grand Hotel.

Duncan wasn't on the ledge between the front hall and the living room, where he usually sat waiting. He wasn't on his perch, either.

"Where's the birdie, Prima?" she asked, pulling her hat over her eyes as she walked through the house. The living room had cheap dark panelling that was at least 50 years old, an ornate gold brocade couch, a brown tweed recliner, and carpet in a green and orange shag. Bob probably never changed a thing after moving in.

Suddenly there was a squawk and a swish, and she instinctively raised her arm to shield her head from Duncan as he dove from the top of a bookcase.

"Hussy," he shrieked. "Go home."

He landed on the dining room table in front of her. Prima leaned out of her arms and unleashed a machine gun fire of high-pitched yaps. It sounded like she was telling Duncan in no uncertain terms to back off. Surprisingly, the bird did just that. He hopped away, saying, "Oopsie. Oopsie." Finally, he jumped onto his perch, fluttered his wings and settled down.

"Thanks, Prima," she said, as the little dog continued to stare at Duncan. "Keep that up and you'll be my ride or die girl."

For the next half hour, she went from room to room with Prima in her arms, taking stock. Bob had really only used the living room, kitchen and one bedroom, but there were six bedrooms in all, and three bathrooms. Long ago, this place had housed large families that tended a proper working farm. Over the past few decades, owners had sold off most of the land; only the fields to the east were still cultivated. Bob leased the land to a farmer in the next county, bringing in enough to cover the property taxes.

The house was run-down, but it had good bones. It wouldn't take a huge investment to turn it into a small inn, or a large bed and breakfast. She could still keep a place downtown to get away from it all.

"Just brainstorming," she said, heading back outside to wait on the porch. "Don't get your hopes up too much, Prima."

A dust cloud in the distance told her the posse was approaching.

Bridget's green van pulled up in front of the house and the side panel opened. Six women spilled out of the back: Duff, Maisie, Nika, Sasha Wildwood, Ari and Remi. During her recent visits, Hannah had met the entire Mafia, both core members and peripheral. The group practically burst with personality, and every single one of them was striking. She wondered if the air in Dorset Hills just made everyone more attractive, or maybe she just noticed people more without the hustle and bustle of city life.

"All hands on deck," Cori called, as she hopped down from the passenger seat. "Short straw mucks the stalls."

"I'm not mucking stalls," Duff said. "Not in these shoes."

"You do everything in heels," Bridget said, stepping back so that Beau could jump out of the van.

Prima struggled to get down from Hannah's arms and then shot toward Beau, yapping ferociously. The big black dog simply stepped aside and pretended not to notice her. It took the wind right out of her sails.

Cori waved one gloved hand. "Care to join us, Hannah? Don't you want to learn how to feed your own livestock?"

"Not particularly," Hannah said. "But I don't want them to starve, either."

"No cows starve on my watch," Cori said. "Time for Livestock 101."

Hannah fell in step with Bridget and Beau. "How does a dog trainer know so much about all of this?" she asked.

"Cori's been hiring herself out to any business with animals since she graduated," Bridget said. "So when she says she knows it all, it's usually true."

"*Always* true," Cori said, circling back to join them. "And let me tell you, a good livestock manager is very hard to find these days."

Hannah's heart sank. "Really?"

"The City's been phasing out farming for decades," Cori said. "Council bought a lot of land, rezoned it, and then sold it to developers. They've outbid anyone who has an interest in agriculture. True farmers have moved north and east, away from the hills."

Bridget nodded. "Sullivan says the only reason Runaway Farm has avoided the wrecking ball is that Bob was well-connected. That, and the fact the land technically used to be split along county lines. For a long time, it belonged to Wolff County. It transferred over to Dorset Hills about 30 years ago, but Bob never worried till Bill Bradshaw took office."

"Developers," Cori muttered.

"My boyfriend is one of the top developers in this city," Bridget reminded her. "They don't make the decisions on what gets built. And it's not their fault the city is growing so fast. The Dog Town branding has worked too well."

Cori rolled her eyes. "You didn't used to talk like that... before sexy Sully."

Beau's hackles went up as he sensed tension between the women. "It's okay, Beau," Bridget said, resting her fingers on his head. "Cori and I can agree to disagree on this, because we agree on almost everything else."

Clenching gloved hands into fists, Cori sighed. "I like Sullivan as a person. But I hate what development is doing to this town."

"Again, we agree." Bridget's voice was calm and Beau nudged Cori's gloved hand, almost apologetically.

Unclenching her fist, Cori touched the dog's head. "It's alright, buddy. When the chips are down, she's the boss, and I'm just your trainer."

Inside the barn, everyone waited for Cori's direction and the commands came thick and fast. Many hands made light work, and soon the horse, cows and sheep were watered and fed. Cori and Maisie mucked out the stalls, while Sasha, the owner of a grooming salon, collected eggs from the chicken coop. Her face lit up like a kid at Easter as she filled a basket lined with foam cups.

"Look at this," she said, offering the basket to show brown, white, and gray eggs in various sizes, some with pretty speckles. "So pretty. There are nearly 40 eggs."

"I'm going to deliver them to the neighbors," Hannah said. "Just like Bob did."

"Gonna take the horse?" Cori asked. She gestured to an antique cart in one corner of the barn. "I could probably hook that up for you."

"I do ride, you know." Hannah patted a saddle that hung on a hook on the wall. "But I'm afraid the eggs would arrive scrambled."

"If they arrived at all." Cori stroked the horse between its ears. "Florence is blind now."

Hannah went over to the horse. "Seriously? Why didn't Fox mention that? If she loved these animals as much as everyone says, she could have left a cheat sheet when she quit."

"That was probably against the terms of her deal with the devil," Cori said.

"The mayor must have offered her something big to leave you in the lurch like that," Bridget said.

"If my sources are correct, he did indeed," Cori said.

"Your sources are always good," Remi said, checking to make sure Leo and Prima were still poking around in dusty corners. "So what does all this mean?"

Cori flexed her hands. "War. That's what it means. Mayor Bradshaw has taken his first shot across the bow. Now we start evasive maneuvers."

There was a general groan among the women.

"Not again," Sasha said. "It's only been three months since the City targeted my grooming salon."

"And a month since he took a bead on dog breeders," Ari said. "We're still waiting to see what he does with those regulations."

"It's a game of whack-a-mole with this mayor," Duff said. "Just when you've got him down, he pops up again, worse than ever."

"How are we going to find a new farm manager?" Remi asked. "No one wants to flout the mayor blatantly."

"Except me," Cori said. "And maybe a few of my friends. I can find you a couple of leads, Hannah. Trust no one I haven't thoroughly vetted, okay?"

A shadow fell across the doorway and they all jumped. "Ladies, relax." It was Sally Taylor, her next-door neighbor

—if a mile away counted as next door. Sally's golf cart sat right outside but no one had heard its quiet purr. She held a clear plastic container filled with muffins. "I brought breakfast," she said. "Made with your very own eggs, Hannah."

"How lovely," Hannah said. "I'll put on a pot of coffee and we can all relax."

"We're not done, here," Cori said. "The sheep paddock needs to be raked out."

"I'll do it," Sally said. "I've done it before. But where's Fox? She hardly ever takes a day off."

"She resigned, I'm afraid," Hannah said. "As did the part-timers."

"Really?" Sally held the muffins in one hand and rested the other on her hip. "She loved these animals. What happened?"

"No idea," Hannah said. "She just left me a note in the door and disappeared."

"Well, then, you're definitely going to need an extra set of hands." Sally handed the muffins to Remi and then reached for a shovel. Florence nickered as Sally passed and she pulled a sugar cube out of her pocket and offered it to her on the palm of her hand. "I'll help out till you find someone. The work keeps me in shape."

Hannah looked to Cori, who gave a single nod. Sally was apparently on the side of good.

"Thank you so much, Sally," Hannah said. "I'll pay whatever you think is fair, and I promise it won't be too long."

"Never mind that," Sally said, patting Hannah's shoulder just as she had the horse's neck. "We're all family here. And you know how families are."

"Speaking of warfare," Cori said, grinning.

There was a general murmur of agreement, and then

Duff's voice rose above everyone else's. "We help each other out, and then we break bread together. Or in this case, muffins."

"No sharp knives, please," Cori said, as they left the barn.

CHAPTER SIX

"First thing I'm going to do when I get a day off is go shopping," Hannah said the next morning as she mucked out the horse stall. Her arms and shoulders still ached from the day before. Although she was fit, farm work used muscles she didn't know she had. "I never thought I'd say this, but I need a pair of denim overalls and some work boots. Turns out my jeans were meant for clubbing not mucking. And my sneakers... well, they're toast."

Florence offered a snort and Prima didn't even look up from her patrol of the barn's corners. Bob had said that like most terriers, Prima was a gifted ratter. Hannah didn't want proof of that.

When the stall was clean, she moved Florence back inside, and then pushed the wheelbarrow to the outside pen. Flies lifted in a swarm as she started tossing their breakfast into the manure bin.

That was when the first wave of nausea hit her. She leaned over the fence into the manure pile. The stench seemed to infiltrate her entire body, and her own breakfast made a sudden and decisive exit.

Prima came out of the barn and stared up at her. "It's okay, girl," she said, pushing strands of hair off her damp forehead. "I'm just not used to the fresh farm air."

When she felt steady, she left the wheelbarrow, grabbed her bottle of water, and sat on a bench in the shade. Her reaction to the odor was strange. She'd taken riding lessons as a girl, and manure had never bothered her before.

"It's stress," she told the dog, who jumped up beside her. "You want to know something, Prima? People think having money means you have nothing to worry about. I've got more worries now than when I was broke and working in a community agency."

She'd enjoyed that job and a carefree life, even living with roommates. Her mom had wanted her to pursue a more creative career, and her dad had tried to entice her into the family business, but she'd made her own choices. For a time, she'd seen little of her parents because of that. When her mom got ill, however, she'd put Hannah in charge of her estate, and there'd never truly been a carefree moment since. Spending her mom's fortune wisely was a responsibility that had drained much of the fun out of life. Unfortunately, the rift with her father that began after college only worsened when her mom got sick, and hadn't yet fully healed. Maybe it never would now that she'd come home to Dorset Hills. He'd think less of her for returning to the town he'd disliked and her mom had loved. It had been one of many points of contention between them.

Prima gave a little whine, and climbed into her lap. Running a hand over the dog's bristly fur, Hannah took a few deep breaths. Here, the scent of wildflowers reached her. A gentle wind cooled her face. "It's going to be okay," she said. "The world will flip right side up again. It always does. All I've got to do is hold on tight for a bit."

A haze of dust on the driveway signalled Sally's arrival. She had a red bandana over her gray hair and an orange one covering her nose and mouth. Rolling to a gentle stop, she pulled the orange cloth down to reveal a grin.

"I saw your lips moving," she said. "You're talking to that dog, aren't you?"

Hannah grinned back at her. "She's a good listener."

"Bob thought the world of her," Sally said, climbing out of the golf cart. "He'd be thrilled she likes you." Prima growled deep in her chest and Sally shrugged. "She's never liked me, that's for sure."

"Just lucky, I guess." Hannah set the dog on the ground, and walked over. "Sally, do you think I could try driving your golf cart?"

"Well, sure, kid," she said. "But you look a little green around the gills if I'm honest. Are you sure you want to add stops and starts to that?"

"I'm fine. Just getting used to the fine bouquet of farm living."

"Suit yourself. The key's always in the transmission."

Slipping into the seat, Hannah said, "Okay, how does it work?"

"Easy-peasy. Accelerator on the right. Brake on the left. Just tap lightly and you'll be good. It only goes 15 miles per hour, floored."

Sliding her hands over the small steering wheel, Hannah said, "It feels very manageable."

"Nearly a thousand pounds, though," Sally said. "Don't run over my feet."

Hannah laughed. "Why not a real car? You can't take this into town for groceries."

"I drive to the general store and back on one charge,"

Sally said. "My old beater was burning money so I picked this up secondhand."

"You take this on the highway? Is that legal?"

"Never bothered to check," she said. "Some drivers are jerks, but I just wave for them to go around me."

"Maybe I'll scoot out to the road and back," Hannah said. "Slowly."

"Wait'll you get a taste of freedom," Sally said. "No more drivers and cabs. No more flak from people like Cori."

"It's like training wheels. I'll master a golf cart, and then a real car won't be so daunting."

"Stop talking and get it, girl."

Sliding forward, Hannah pressed the accelerator lightly with her right sneaker. The purring golf cart took a little hop.

"Just tap it," Sally said.

"Tap it," Hannah repeated, giving the pedal a quick jab with her foot. It lurched forward, and she turned the wheel. The golf cart spun more quickly than she expected and cut so close to Sally that she jumped back. Pulling hard on the wheel, Hannah corrected course and started up the driveway. "Stay, Prima," she called over her shoulder.

The dust whirled up so that when she looked over her shoulder the entire farm was obscured. But the way ahead was clear and she pressed harder till she was going full out. It may have only been 15 miles per hour, but it did feel like freedom. Near the high iron sign, she let out a little whoop and turned the cart in a tight circle. Then she did it again. The tie slipped out of her hair and long strands whipped across her eyes.

That was probably how she missed the pickup truck turning into the driveway. There was a crunch of gravel, and when her cart turned back toward the road, it was just in time to see the big truck fishtail and come to an abrupt stop. The red pickup was close enough for her to feel a wave of heat, and the two clouds of dust—one great, one small— merged. She screamed, punching wildly with her foot for the brake. Finding it at last, she pressed. The cart slowed, but not quite enough. Instead, she ran headfirst into the stationary truck. There was a crunch of metal on metal, and she screamed again, gasped and then choked on dust.

A muffled shout reached her, which got louder as the truck's door opened. A man yelled, "Are you alright?" as feet thumped toward her.

"I'm fine, I'm fine," she said, coughing. "I am so sorry. I should never have— Oh. Nick. Hi."

"You sure you're not hurt? You may have whiplash." His brow furrowed and his dark eyes were full of concern. "Hannah, I offered to teach you to drive in a real vehicle."

She smiled in spite of herself. "You really think I'm capable of handling your truck?"

"My sister's car is perfect for jobs like this." He ran his hand over the fender, and winced.

"I'll pay for repairs, of course," Hannah said.

"It's okay. It's barely a scratch. What are fenders for?" But he pressed his lips together to keep from saying more.

"Nick, I feel terrible. It's like a pet, isn't it?"

"No, no. Don't be silly. It's nothing like what I feel for my dog." Forcing a smile, he added, "Nothing stays new for long, right?"

Climbing out of the golf cart, she sighed. "Some people just aren't meant to pilot moving vehicles. Would you drive it back, please? I need a few minutes to think about how I'll tell Sally I dented her cart. In my own driveway."

He shook his head. "Get right back on the horse, lady. I'll walk you through it."

In fact, he ran her through it, jogging beside the cart and shouting directions like a drill sergeant. "Brake. Speed up. Brake. Turn to the right. Slow-slow-slow. Straighten out. Speed up. STOP."

He barked the last order just as Prima shot toward them. The dog ignored him completely and leapt into Hannah's lap.

"She's really taken to you," Nick said.

The dog writhed as if Hannah had been gone for hours, rather than 15 minutes. "Who wouldn't?" she said. "I'm a farm dog's dream come true."

"Who wouldn't?" Nick echoed. He reached over to pet Prima and pulled his hand back fast when she flashed teeth. "Wow. A guard terrier."

"Every girl needs one," Hannah said. Then she stared the dog down and said, "Leave it, Prima."

Nick leaned to peer under the cart's roof. She hadn't realized he was quite that tall. Nor had she noticed how white his teeth were. Or that his eyes were a beautiful shade of hazel, rather than brown. Not that these things mattered. Not at all. She must be addled from the collision.

"I'd better let you go," she said, although it was Nick who'd slung one arm over the roof of the golf cart. "Actually, I never asked why you're here."

"Remi told me you'd lost your staff and needed a hand," he said. "I had the day off and wanted to help out."

"She's covered." Sally's voice made them both jump. She was inside the barn but obviously had a good sightline. "But thanks, handsome."

Heat rose in Hannah's cheeks. "Sally Taylor, my wonderful neighbor, volunteered to sling manure today. But I really appreciate the offer, Nick. People have been so kind."

Nick lowered his voice. "Well, I heard about your farm manager getting bought off. It's really not fair." He turned to look at the barn before continuing. "Speaking of fair... did you know the Dorset Hills spring fair kicks off tomorrow? I wondered if you'd like to go."

She stared up at those hazel eyes, and felt her resistance melting. "I wish I could, Nick, but I'm so busy here right now."

"She'd love to," Sally called. "Name the date and I'll make sure I'm free to babysit the menagerie."

Nick's teeth gleamed again. "That sounds promising."

"Maybe she won't be so kind when she sees the front of her cart," Hannah said.

Gesturing for him to follow, she pulled the golf cart forward, almost to the front porch. Getting out, she set Prima on the seat she'd vacated and the dog curled up. "It's so sweet of you to ask about the fair, Nick, but I'm going to have to say no."

His smile faded at the same moment a cloud concealed the sun. "You don't like fairs? Or you're seeing someone?"

"Neither. I'm just not in a position to date at the moment. All I want to do is focus on getting Runaway Farm sorted out. After what happened with the mayor yesterday, I'm not even sure I want to stay in Dorset Hills long term. So there's no point getting entrenched."

"No problem," Nick said, dropping it. "I completely understand. But before you go anywhere, promise you'll let me teach you how to drive."

His smile came back out and warmed her like sunshine. He was a gentleman, no doubt about that. "I'll think about it, thanks."

"Think hard," he said. "Driving is a life-changer."

His eyes locked on hers again and her throat tightened.

It was a shame she couldn't go driving with a nice guy like Nick. But that wasn't in the cards for her now. There were too many complications—things that made farming look easy.

A horn blared suddenly and broke the spell. Down the driveway, behind Nick's truck, sat another pickup, this one black. The driver's door opened and a gray head emerged.

"Coming through," the old man shouted. "Heard there was a damsel in distress here."

CHAPTER SEVEN

The Ferris wheel sent out a glittering, revolving message that the first official spring fair in Dorset Hills had begun. Technically, the location was just outside city limits, but there was no open space large enough to hold the assortment of fun park rides, games, food trucks and other vendors, not to mention a stage for the biggest bands the City could attract.

Mayor Bradshaw had attended the ribbon cutting earlier that day, taken a ride on the dog-themed carousel, and posed for portraits with dozens of children and dogs. Remi had managed to get a copy of his schedule from a contact at City Hall so that they could be sure not to run into him. It was the only way to get Cori to agree to attend, and her vocal disgust over the whole affair would add greatly to everyone's enjoyment. Like the rest of the group, Hannah had quickly come to appreciate Cori's outspokenness. You paid a price for it with occasional painful jabs, but then you got to enjoy it the other 95 percent of the time.

Today, Cori was in Hannah's good books because

Charlie Garnett, the farm manager she'd recommended, had accepted the job. The panic that had been fluttering constantly in her chest had simmered down for the moment.

"Someone tell me why we needed a spring fair," Cori asked, rubbing her eyes with balled up gloves. "This is making my head hurt. Why isn't this money going to valuable services for pets in need? Or any other worthy cause, for that matter."

"Community spirit," Duff said. "Mayor Bradshaw knows full well he'd never get elected if he were running today. His way of turning public opinion in his favor has always been a flashy event. Remember the party in Bellington Square at New Year's? Marti Forrester told me he brought in that merry-go-round from Kansas City."

Bridget's frown deepened as she stared at people riding around and around on figurines shaped like different dog breeds. "Imagine what that kind of money could do to care for and rehabilitate rescues. Instead we ship strays to neighboring counties and pay for silly rides."

"I wish they had one of those dunking booths," Cori said, flexing her fingers. "I'd pay a good price to drop the mayor in the drink."

Sasha laughed. "There'd be a fistfight in line as everyone tried to go first. They could auction the dunk shot to the highest bidder for a good cause."

Hannah laughed along with the rest, but like Remi, she couldn't help smiling as she looked around. Sure, it was silly and costly, but it was hard not to like a county fair on a lovely spring evening, especially when dogs were not only permitted but honored guests. There were agility courses, pools and fenced play areas for the dogs to burn off steam. Prima's manners weren't reliable enough to allow her to attend events like this yet, but Hannah had asked Cori to work with her on obedience. Leo was there and standing on his four white paws, as he usually was when Cori was around to reprimand Remi. Beau, Bridget's elegant shadow, showed no interest at all in attractions other dogs would enjoy. He always struck Hannah as being more of a guardian spirit than a real dog.

Remi slowed and tugged on Hannah's sleeve until they fell behind the group. "Why did you turn down Nick Springdale?" she asked. "It would have been the perfect Dog Town first date."

"And miss girls' night at the fair? No way." Hannah snatched a handful of Remi's popcorn and grinned. "Cori's more fun than Nick could ever be."

"I don't know about that," Remi said. "Correction: I do know about that. Tiller is plenty of fun. I get the best of both worlds, because he's coming later, for the band. You could have had a plus-one, too. From what I've seen, Nick is a stand-up guy and a sweetheart. Not to mention pretty easy on the eyes."

"No argument there," Hannah said. "He's also a very good brother to Evie. Seeing them together around Easter made me miss James. He was supposed to be home from Europe by now. I wonder if he's met some girl."

Remi lifted Leo under one arm as a rambunctious Rottweiler headed their way. Handing the popcorn to Hannah, she said, "That'd be good, right? To see James matched up?"

"Of course. Yeah. He deserves the best."

"I'm sure he'd say the same of you."

Hannah nodded, staring back at the carousel. The only terrier in the collection was a Scottie. "He would and he has."

Remi put Leo in Hannah's arms and reclaimed the popcorn. This move had played out so often that Hannah barely noticed the dog's arrival. She hugged him automatically, never looking away from the ride.

"What kind of guy are you looking for? If they're not wealthy, it must be hard for them to even approach you. A woman who has money can be hard on their egos, I suppose, even today."

"It's not that," Hannah said. "I was raised without much money and often I feel uncomfortable having so much given to me. I certainly don't need a wealthy man."

"Then what are you waiting for?" Remi leaned in closer and whispered. "Does this have anything to do with what happened in high school?"

Hannah's eyes flashed to meet her friend's and then she shook her head. "What happened at prom probably affected my previous relationships, but it's not about that now."

"What then? I could have sworn I sensed some chemistry between you and Nick."

They'd lost the others by now, and ended up in a long row of games. Guys were giving their best shots at ring toss, darts and hoops to win stuffed animals for their dates, and the girls giggled, squealed, and hopped up and down. Hannah knew she'd never feel that untroubled again, and it brought tears to her eyes. Life had changed forever the year before, through no fault of her own. Now she carried a burden that she blocked pretty well most of the time.

"I'm not sure I know what chemistry feels like anymore," she said at last. "It's been a few years."

"But you said you wanted to settle down and raise a family before long. Or have you changed your mind?"

Remi was nothing if not persistent. It seemed like every

word that had dropped from people's lips was catalogued and stored for later use. She was some kind of savant.

Burying her face in Leo's silky coat, Hannah shook her head. "I'd love to have a family. I'm just not sure it's possible."

"Why wouldn't it be possible?"

"Remi, can we just enjoy the fair?" Hannah asked. "Please?"

"Of course. Sorry." Remi turned her worried eyes away from Hannah, to give her a moment. At a nearby booth, a man pushed the huge stuffed bear he'd won into his date's hands and she hugged it, laughing. Then she stood on tiptoe and kissed his cheek. The young man's eyes shone—as if that one teddy bear had saved the world from imminent demise.

"It's all a game of chance," Remi said. "All we can do is look before we leap and hope for the best."

Hannah's wavy dark hair dusted Leo as she nodded again. "I guess you're right."

"There are no guarantees in life, unless you decide to sit on the bench. That's a guarantee of nothing ever happening." She tried to pry Leo out of Hannah's arms and failed. "Let's throw bean bags through hoops. You win, I get off your back. I win, you go out with Nick."

Lowering Leo to the grass, Hannah managed a smile. "I commit to nothing except whipping your butt."

Soon they were laughing as they tossed beanbags at the hoops. When one set ran out, they bought more, and stayed stuck at a tie for the longest time. Finally, Remi managed to land the winning shot.

"I win," Remi said. "Thank goodness."

"Like you'd get off my back anyway," Hannah said.

They turned at the sound of a familiar voice. A few

yards away, Nick Springdale was tossing darts at a life-sized cardboard image of a man that bore a passing resemblance to the mayor. Beside him, a pretty blonde woman cheered him on.

Remi and Hannah stood watching until the young man in the booth handed over a large stuffed beagle to Nick, who in turn passed it to the woman. She stood on her toes and tried to kiss him, but he moved at the last minute.

Turning, Hannah walked away. "I guess I double lose," she said.

"But you said you didn't want him," Remi said, following her.

"Even more so now."

"That wasn't a date, I'm sure of it," Remi said. "I don't know the woman... and I pretty much know everyone."

"So he's importing," Hannah said. "And like Duncan, he prefers blondes."

"In case you didn't notice, that kiss didn't land," Remi said. "I'm quite sure he can still be yours... if you actually want him. Do you?"

Hannah ignored her question and headed into an area full of large metal enclosures. "Why do they have livestock here when it's practically banned by the city?"

"Because it's technically Wolff County land," Remi said. "It was probably a condition of agreeing to let us use the space. Tomorrow there will be prizes for best in show and a lot will sell."

They walked among the pens, looking at cows, sheep, goats, and large cages containing even more breeds of chickens that Hannah hadn't seen. In most enclosures, the owner sat on a folding chair, trying to catch their eyes to sell them on the virtues of their particular animal. At the end of the row was a pen holding just one pig. She was thoroughly encrusted with dirt. Even so, Hannah could tell she was skin and bones, at least by pig standards. The sow's small pinkish eyes were mucky and one ear was torn. Her head hung so low her nose almost touched the ground and she was completely still.

"This pig looks awful," Hannah said. "What's it doing here?"

The man sitting in the next pen with his goat spoke up. "Owner's trying to sell her. She's not producing like he wants."

Tears welled up in Hannah's eyes. "That's terrible. If she's not producing it's because she's starving, I'm sure. You're not supposed to see a pig's ribs."

The man shrugged. "Tell it to him, not me."

"I will tell it to him," Hannah said. "Where is he?"

"Last I heard he was in the tavern." He jerked a thumb toward the only tent that served alcohol. "Name's Jerry. Black wool hat and beard to match. Don't tell him I told you."

Equally outraged, Remi charged ahead of Hannah, pulling Leo so fast he whined in protest. Prying open Remi's fingers, Hannah took the leash away, and then lifted Leo into her arms.

"Slow down," she said. "We'll find this guy. But we'll make a better case if we look chill when we get there."

Remi stopped suddenly in front of a booth, where a woman was sitting surrounded on three walls by paintings and sketches. A small white dog with one black ear sat on her lap, and a goldendoodle lay on the grass beside her, next to a stack of hardcover books.

"Hey Remi," the woman said, lifting her pencil from her sketchbook. "What's up?"

"We're going to see a man about a pig," Remi said.

"There's a neglected sow in a pen and its owner is apparently in the beer tent enjoying some beverages."

The woman held out her hand to Hannah. "I'm Flynn Strathmore. We met at the Easter festival."

"Of course. You're a wonderful artist," Hannah said. "I've followed your work for years."

"I've got nothing on your mom," Flynn said, smiling. "She's still an inspiration to me."

Hannah looked down at Leo. Even six years later, it was difficult to hear about her mom without crying. Normally she just changed the subject, and she tried it now. "Would you watch Leo for us for a few minutes while we deal with our pig problem?"

Flynn accepted Leo's leash and Hannah led Remi into the beer tent. The place was filled with long tables and benches. There were so many men with dark hats and beards that it seemed unlikely they'd ever find Jerry, the owner of the neglected pig.

A few dozen pairs of eyes turned toward them and some low whistles rang out.

"Oh no," Remi said. "Maybe we should—"

"Jerry?" Hannah called out. "We're looking for Jerry, owner of the sow in pen 38. Where are you Jerry?"

A hand came up, somewhat tentatively. "Who's asking?"

Hannah picked her way through the benches, with Remi close behind her. "I'd like to speak to you about your pig," she said, when they reached him.

"What about her?" Jerry's eyes didn't meet hers. They didn't actually rise past her chest.

"I noticed she's not well," Hannah said. "She's very thin. And her skin is a mess. Did you notice the rash?"

Jerry's eyes shifted from Hannah's chest to her chin. "And you are?"

"A concerned citizen," Hannah said. "Someone who cares about suffering animals."

"She's not suffering." Jerry's voice spiked. "What do you know?"

"I know she looked sad," Hannah said. "Depressed."

"Sad?" Jerry shook his head. "Lady, we're talking about a pig, not a baby."

Some of the men laughed and elbowed each other. Hannah's face started to burn. She wasn't used to being happy hour entertainment.

"Do you hear that?" A guy across the table cupped his ear. "Someone's clock is ticking."

Remi pushed forward. "Excuse me? How dare you!"

"Oops, there's another one, Jer." The other man looked nearly identical except his cap was plaid, with ear flaps. "Tick tock."

"Look, lady," Jerry said. "Take your livestock lecture somewhere else. You're out of your league."

The heat in Hannah's face burned through the last of her composure. "I know a miserable pig when I see one," she said.

Ear Flaps guffawed at that, and color also rose in Jerry's face. He squinted up at Hannah and growled, "You don't know squat about pigs, princess."

Remi must have felt an explosion coming, because she squeezed Hannah's arm tight and whispered, "Don't, Hannah."

"Hannah?" Ear Flaps said. Then he leaned over and whispered something to Jerry.

"Right." Jerry swung his leg over the bench to scan Hannah up and down from close range. "You're the one who rode into Dorset Hills on her high horse and took advantage of a dying man."

Hannah's throat went dry, but when he started to speak, she held up her hand. "Jerry, you've said enough."

"You're a know-it-all rich b—"

The last word was cut off by a sharp yelp. Hannah had set the heel of her new work boot firmly on his shoe and pressed. She was sad that she wasn't wearing stilettos but happy Jerry was wearing sneakers.

Before he could recover his voice, she said, "Bob Hess sold me that farm because he knew my mother. Not that I owe you, or anyone else, an explanation."

"That doesn't make you a pig expert," Ear Flaps said, since Jerry had lost his words.

"I intend to become one," Hannah said. "That's why I'm offering a very fair price for a sick pig."

"She's not for sale." Jerry swung his leg over the bench and turning his back. "Not to you."

"Every pig has its price," Hannah said.

"Don't be stupid, Jer," Ear Flaps said. "Take her money and buy the next round."

"Yeah, don't be stupid, Jer," Hannah said. "You can take a point too far, you know."

"Hannah," Remi tried again. "You really *can* take a point too far."

Shushing her with a wave, Hannah leaned over. "I can tell you're a smart business man, Jerry. Take my money. You're also getting a great story about how you bilked the rich girl."

Jerry stared up at her, his small eyes calculating. Finally he gave a quick nod.

"I'll expect delivery to Runaway Farm tomorrow," she said.

He sat down and turned his back. "Send your limo, princess. I don't deliver."

FLYNN BARELY LOOKED up as her right hand moved swiftly across the sketchbook when they joined her again. "Did you give him a piece of your mind?"

"She gave him more than that," Remi said, smiling.

Flynn's eyes rose from the sketch. "You did not buy a pig, Hannah Pemberton."

"There was no way I was leaving her with that loser," Hannah said. "Not when there's room at Runaway Farm."

"That's probably how Bob went bankrupt," Remi said, grinning. "Cori is going to be proud of you."

Hannah found that thought more comforting that she expected. "Good. Because we're going to need some help to get that pig home. It won't fit in your car."

Flynn ripped a page out of her sketchbook and handed it to Hannah. "Here's what I saw while you were gone."

Remi gasped and clasped her hands. "Flynn's a prophetic artist, you know. What she draws comes true."

"Sometimes it takes a little imagination," Flynn said.

On the page was a baby stroller, out of which emerged a mitten, or perhaps a cloven hoof. A tall man pushed the stroller, and beside it trotted a terrier that looked exactly like Prima. The only dot of color was the small pink mitten.

Hannah stared at the drawing. "Is that a baby girl, or devil's spawn?" she asked.

Looking over her shoulder, Remi said, "It's a pig's hoof, I think."

Flynn shrugged. "You got back too soon. Interrupted my

flow. All I can tell you is I saw a hot guy, a stroller and a scrappy little dog. Take it or leave it."

Hannah rolled up the drawing carefully and slipped it into her bag. "I'll take it," Hannah said, grinning. "If it turns out to be devil's spawn, I'll return it for a new one."

CHAPTER EIGHT

The sun was clawing its way over the horizon when the cab driver left Hannah at Runaway Farm the next morning.

"The place looks abandoned," he said. "You sure you're okay alone?"

"I'm not alone," she said, letting Prima jump out ahead of her. The dog raced in a huge circle, yipping with joy. She tolerated the hotel surprisingly well, but her heart was clearly on the farm. "There's always a crowd here."

Aladdin, the rooster, was raising his voice to greet the day. The rest of the menagerie was making species-specific noises that blurred into an excited cacophony. Her arrival meant freedom for most and breakfast for all.

As the cab headed back out to the highway, she sighed. Despite the crowd, she *did* feel alone here. Hopefully Charlie Garnett, the manager Cori had recommended, would work out. Today was his first day and she wanted to be on hand to welcome him. If all went as planned he could take over the day-to-day grind, giving her a chance to find a home in the city and create a long-term strategy for the farm. She also needed to contact the part-time candidates Cori and Charlie had suggested to make sure there was plenty of backup.

Duncan's tune had changed dramatically, and quite literally, in just a few days. Now when he saw her he made a musical purring sound. Today, he called out, "Oooh la la," the moment she turned the lights on. He hopped from the ledge by the door to the coffee table and over to the recliner, fluttering his wings in what seemed like an invitation.

"What's gotten into you?" she asked. "Are you a lonely bird? Maybe we need to find you a lassie."

"Hello, Lassie," he said, still fluttering near the recliner. "Whatcha doing?"

"Getting you and Prima some breakfast and then heading down to feed the troops."

"Crackers," he said. "Crackers."

Hannah rubbed her stomach. "Not even crackers for me. I've been queasy since the moment I set foot on this land. I think I have a bad case of the mayors."

Once she'd doled out their meals, she put on a pot of coffee and reluctantly opened the door to Bob's bedroom. Remi and Mim had cleared out most of his personal belongings, but she remembered seeing denim overalls hanging from a hook in the closet. There were a few T-shirts still in the drawer, so she changed quickly, tucking the T-shirt deep into the overalls and rolling up the pant legs. There were stains down the bib that looked rusty, like faded blood, and a triangular tear in one leg. They'd have to do for now. She wanted Charlie to think she was not only engaged, but also capable of keeping the place afloat. No doubt he'd report back to Cori on her every wrong move.

His truck rolled up as she poured coffee into two travel mugs. Stuffing packets of sugar and creamer into her bib pocket, she hurried out onto the porch. The sun had succeeded in pulling itself clear of the horizon and was already chasing the chill away.

"Morning," Charlie called, jumping out and waiting for her by the truck. "Ready to show me the ropes?" He waited for her mouth to drop and then laughed. "Let me rephrase that... Ready to let me show *you* the ropes?"

"Funny," she said, handing him a coffee mug. "You're a funny man, Charlie."

"I agree," he said. "I think my humor was wasted in the insurance business."

Charlie had told her he grew up on a farm about 50 miles away, and still spent his vacations helping out the brother who'd kept the family business going. But Charlie had earned his living—and an early retirement—working in the corporate office of the biggest insurance company in hill country. He'd been planning to leave that summer and Cori convinced him to use up vacation time to escape early.

Leading the way into the barn, Charlie beamed as if he'd landed in the villa of his dreams. With his silver hair and bright blue eyes behind wire-rimmed glasses, he was handsome, and she wondered about his backstory. Was he divorced? A widower? Or a ladies' man who'd never settled down? His smile was warm, but not so warm that she felt comfortable asking personal questions.

"Cori's coming around nine," she said. "With the pig."

His salt and pepper eyebrows soared. "Pig? What pig?"

"The one I bought last night at the fair," she mumbled into her coffee cup. "It was neglected. Starving. I couldn't leave it."

Charlie shook his head. "You can't just bring any old animal on board, Ms. Pemberton."

"Hannah. Please. And why not? A pig's a farm animal. It's a farm."

"A hobby farm. There's a difference. The footprint here is technically pretty small. You don't just jam animals together. Not if you want them to be happy. Each one has its own needs and wants."

"Well, I needed and wanted to rescue that sow," she said. "Please tell me there's room for her."

His expression softened. "We can make it work. We'll need more pasture fenced off. The sheep need more room, anyway. And the pig can go in the back for now. Sows can be pretty ornery, in case you don't know."

"She seemed sweet," Hannah said. "I'm calling her Wilma. After Wilber in Charlotte's Web."

"Of course. Wilma." He laughed as he went over to the big sink and turned on the faucet to fill a bucket. "Let's get you set up with instructions. I'll tell you exactly what I'm doing, and in what order, so that you'll know how to manage the place on your own."

"On my own?" Her throat tightened. "You're staying, right?"

"As long as I'm on the right side of the grass," he said. "Any idea how many people drop dead right after they retire? You learn these things in the insurance business."

"Those are people without a purpose, I bet. You have a purpose."

"That I do." He peered at her over his glasses. "I have big plans for my second inning."

Before she could question him in detail about his plans, she heard the sound of tires on gravel. Bridget's green van was backing right up to the wide barn doors.

Charlie waved both arms as he walked around the side of the van. Cori was behind the wheel, with Bridget in the passenger seat. She rolled down the window and said, "This pig is all yours, people. She squealed the entire drive."

"My van will never be the same," Bridget said.

"I'll pay for detailing," Hannah said. "Thank you so much for bringing her."

"Rule number one," Charlie said. "You don't put a new animal in with the old ones until you know she's healthy. So, straight into the back pen she goes. She sleeps in the shed for two weeks even after the vet clears her."

Cori's eyes flashed from him over to Hannah and back. "And we're going to get her into the back pen *how?*"

"I assumed you crazy rescuers had a plan," he said, rolling his eyes.

"You're just as crazy, my man," Cori said. "That day you scaled—"

"Never mind that. I was younger then. And cared less about bending the law."

Cori started to speak and he cut her off. "I've got an idea. We'll bring in the metal dividers from the agility ring and make a chute."

Bridget jumped out and jogged toward the field. "The sooner I get that pig out of my van, the better. Honestly, Hannah. Get your own truck, will you?"

"That'll be the day," Cori said, snickering. "Maybe a trailer for her golf cart."

Hannah flipped Cori the bird, pleased to be quicker at the draw than the tiny trainer. Then she joined Bridget and Charlie, and before long they'd set up a long runway, complete with a steep plank to serve as a ramp from the sliding side panel.

"Someone give Wilma a shove," Charlie said.

"Wilma?" Cori asked.

"Wilma," Hannah said. "I guess I should do the honors."

She started to slide around one of the metal dividers and nearly knocked it over. Cori caught it with one hand. "Stand down, Lady Pemberton. I don't want to be chasing Wilma after you let her escape."

With that, she scaled the divider while Bridget held it steady, and cracked open the van door just enough to slide through. There was some thumping from inside and a couple of loud curses. Wilma was obviously less responsive to Cori's silently expressive gloves than everyone else. Finally, the door opened and a snout appeared.

"Bombs away," Cori called.

Pulling the door back, she planted one boot on Wilma's butt and shoved. The pig barreled down the ramp and continued through the chute, stopping only when it widened into the back pen. Anticipating that, Charlie had jogged ahead and was waving some of the carrots normally reserved for the horse. The underfed pig walked towards him, snuffling eagerly, and once she was chewing, they closed the gate and started breaking things down.

"Is it always going to be like this?" Charlie asked, grinning. "Just one thrill after another?"

Hannah shook her head. "I promise not to buy more livestock without checking with you."

Looking over her shoulder, Charlie gestured. "Better check with *him* first."

The women all turned to see a sleek black sedan pulling up beside them in the parking area. At least, it had been black, before dust from the driveway coated it heavily. The window rolled down and Mayor Bradshaw fanned one elegant hand.

"Good morning all," he called, and then sputtered on

the dust. Fumbling in his jacket, he pulled out a white handkerchief and held it over his mouth. "I come bearing gifts."

Hannah walked over to the car. "How kind, Mayor, but you didn't have to."

"Oh, it's nothing." He passed a small African violet through the window. "Just a token."

"You didn't have to," she repeated. "Really."

"That's not all." He reached for something else on the passenger seat and passed it through the window.

Hannah studied the ornately framed portrait of the mayor. It was a print of the official photo in City Hall. There was a small brass plaque at the bottom with an inscription that appeared to be in Latin. She decided not to ask what it meant. That was what Google translate was for.

"How nice. Thank you." she said. "And what can I do for you today?"

He waved his white handkerchief. "Nothing at all, my dear. I felt like our meeting ended on a sour note the other day and wanted to smooth things over."

"That's kind of you," Hannah said, smiling at last. "I do want to stay on good terms, because I love Dorset Hills."

"I'm glad you still feel that way." Once again, he spoke through the handkerchief. "There are so many options for you in our wonderful town. But first, you'll need to make some decisions about Runaway Farm."

"Decisions? How so?"

Cori stepped in front of the mayor's car and hopped up on the hood as if she belonged there. She leaned back on her hands, both gloves splayed.

"Must she?" the mayor said, gesturing to Cori. When she didn't move, he pressed the heel of his free hand on the horn. The sudden blare didn't startle Cori at all, although

Bridget and Hannah both jumped. Charlie had disappeared, possibly to tend to the pig.

"What exactly did you want to tell me?" Hannah asked.

"So dusty," he said, coughing. "It's like a desert out here."

"It's been quite a dry spell," she said. "Could you regulate more rain?"

He sniffed into the handkerchief. "I wanted you to know that City Council's introduced a new bylaw." His words were muffled. "Owners of hobby farms in Dorset Hills must live on the premises full-time."

Hannah's testy stomach gave another twist. "You said I'm the *only* hobby farm owner in Dorset Hills, so I assume your new bylaw is a direct attack on me."

"Don't think of it that way. Our council is always diligent about closing loopholes." He lowered the handkerchief. "It's for the safety of citizens and animals. We can't be too careful. I'm sure you understand."

Tilting her head, Hannah smiled. "I do understand, sir. Actually, I came to the same conclusion this morning."

His eyes brightened over the white fabric. "Did you, now?"

"I did, indeed. When I got here at dawn—you know, that perfect hour, when everything still feels possible?—I said to myself, 'Hannah, you need to live here. Really live here. Put down roots and grow.'" She waved one arm in a wide arc. "This place is my future."

The kerchief came right down and the light went out of the mayor's eyes. "This dump is— Pardon me. This *place* is your future?"

"I called it a dump myself, but I see its potential now. It could be a resort, or an inn."

"You'll need Council on side for that."

The mayor started to roll up the window. She hooked her fingers, now with three broken nails, over the window's edge, forcing him to stop rolling.

"Why wouldn't Council support an investment in this town?" she asked. "I'd hire locally with local supplies, and ultimately bring tourists in from all over."

"We could do so much more with this land," he said. "Think bigger, Hannah."

The car was still in park, but the mayor pressed down on the gas to make the engine roar. Cori took the hint and hopped off, leaving a distinct butt print on the hood.

"What I need to do, Mayor," Hannah said, "is make my own decisions. That's why I came back to Dorset Hills. It's too hard to make decisions in New York. There's no room to swing a cat."

"That's a terrible expression," Cori said, coming to stand beside Hannah.

The mayor pressed the window button again and Hannah moved her fingers before they could get caught. She raised the portrait and said, "Thanks so much. I'll treasure this."

He put the car in reverse, and Cori bent over to pick up the violet. Running after the car, she set the potted plant on the sedan's hood. They could see his lips pucker as he gently pulled the car around and moved forward at a glacial pace. As far as Hannah could see, the plant stayed in place until he left the property.

HANNAH WAS EMPTYING a bucket of feed over the fence into Wilma's trough when the next wave of nausea hit. She pressed her head against a post and then wretched up the few sips of coffee she'd swallowed earlier.

A big hand clasped her shoulder, and Charlie steered her over to an old stump and pushed her down.

"I'm okay. I'm fine." She wiped her mouth on the back of a work glove. "Bill Bradshaw just makes me sick."

"He has that effect on a lot of people." Charlie watched her for a moment and then turned to dump the rest of the pail into Wilma's trough. "Still, I'm betting there's another reason you're sick."

"Yeah?" She could think of half a dozen reasons, all of them related to this farm. "What's that?"

"You've been green around the gills since I met you," he said. "I'm thinking you and Wilma share the same condition."

"What condition? Malnutrition?"

He glanced back at her and then looked away again. "I've been around enough critters to know Wilma's pregnant. How about you?"

Her lips tried to form words, but nothing came out before she fainted.

CHAPTER NINE

R emi was waiting at the bottom of the trail with one dog under each arm. Her perpetual smile had disappeared behind a cloud of worry, but emerged while Hannah was still a few yards away.

"Congratulations," she said, setting both dogs on the ground and unhooking their leashes. She reaching out to hug her friend as dogs frolicked around their feet. "I'm so happy for you."

"You can read the news on my face?" Hannah said.

"I can." Remi pulled away and nodded. "Obviously the doctor confirmed it, and I can tell you're happy about it."

"Flabbergasted might be a better word. Terrified, for sure."

"And behind that, you're happy. You said you wanted a family. This can't come as a complete shock."

"It is a shock, actually." Hannah snapped her fingers at Prima and started up the trail.

"You don't have to be a farm girl to know how these things happen," Remi said. "Boy meets girl. Boy ravishes girl. Babies ensue."

Hannah laughed. "It's not always that simple."

"The only thing I can't figure out is how all this happened when you said you hadn't dated in years. Were you being coy?"

"Truth," Hannah said.

Remi's eyes scanned the trail ahead, her lips pressed together. "Are you going to let me keep guessing how this miracle happened, or is it too personal?"

"It is personal," Hannah said. "So I'd appreciate it if you'd keep the details private."

"Of course," Remi said. She called the dogs over and hooked them up. "I want to give this my full attention."

Hannah took Prima's leash and walked for a while before she started speaking. "I can hardly believe it. I took a test the day before you asked me to meet you at Runaway Farm. It was negative. I thought that was that."

"Only it wasn't," Remi prompted.

"Home pregnancy tests hardly ever fail, the doctor said. But this one did. I was supposed to see my specialist in New York last week but with all that's gone on, I cancelled my appointment."

"Specialist?" Remi picked Leo up and hugged him, a sure sign she was anxious. "This was planned?"

Hannah nodded. She opened her mouth, and then closed it again.

"Is there a...?" Remi trailed off. "I mean, obviously there is someone."

"There is someone. Technically. But we've never met."

Squeezing Leo till he panted, Remi shook her head. "I don't get it."

Hannah exchanged Prima's leash for Leo, pressing her face into his fur. The beagle smelled better than any dog she'd ever known. It was like he exuded all the love he absorbed.

"I planned this," she said, at last. "On my own. With the help of modern medicine."

"Oh?" Remi said, and then, "*Oh*. Okay. But... why now?"

Hannah's sigh felt pulled right out of the earth through her sneakers. "Time was running out."

"But you're only 34. You have years ahead." Remi clenched her fingers over Prima's leash. "At least, that's what I tell myself."

"Maybe. It gets harder, at least for some of us." Hannah's voice was muffled by Leo. "I just really wanted a family and I didn't want to leave this to chance."

Reaching out, Remi squeezed Hannah's arm. "I couldn't be happier for you. I'm sure you gave it a lot of thought."

At this, Hannah groaned. "Not as much as I should have, probably. It was a bit impulsive."

"How impulsive could it be? It takes ages to plan these things."

"It didn't take all that long, really. That surprised me, too. I thought I'd have more time to get used to the idea." Remi's brow creased, but Hannah raised her hand. "Don't worry, counselling was part of the preparation. I knew what I was doing. It's just that... everything is different in theory."

Now Remi smiled again. "Shiz just got real."

"Exactly. When the result was negative, I was actually relieved. It bought me more time. But it's okay. I still think I'm better moving forward sooner rather than later." Rocking Leo like a baby, she sighed. "I'm just very aware that my mom didn't have as much time as she'd thought. She'd been treated for cancer twice, you know."

"I... I didn't know that. I'm sorry. And I understand how that can give you a different perspective on things."

Hannah offered Leo back and Remi shook her head. "That's the main reason I wanted to move back here—to have a community. If you're going solo with a family, you need to have friends around."

"We're here for you, I promise." Remi churned fingers through her hair until it stood in clumps. "I'm just so sorry now that I pressured you to take over Runaway Farm. You do not need that stress right now."

"Well, I was capable of saying no and sticking to my guns," Hannah said. "Believe it or not, I tell people no every day." She set Leo down and unhooked him, and Remi followed suit with Prima. "Who knows, maybe that's exactly where I'm supposed to be right now. The farm still feels strange and foreign, but not wrong. The only thing that feels wrong is the pressure from the mayor."

"We'll get around him. A dozen clever minds are busy solving the problem of Bill Bradshaw even as we speak."

"And thousands more who voted him in and clearly think he's the cat's pajamas."

They reached Clifford's Crest, the first major plateau with its breathtaking views of the valleys where Dorset Hills and other towns nestled. Even from that elevation, it was obvious that Dog Town was the most prosperous of them, with taller buildings and a larger footprint. Lake Longmuir was a hard stop on one side, but the suburbs spilled out in every other direction. If development continued at its current pace, the city would meet up with neighboring towns in a few years and swallow them. Plowing down Runaway Farm was just one more stepping stone to Dog Town domination.

Prima circled back from the trail and stood beside

Hannah, ears pricked. Her stubby tail stood upright, waving slightly. "What is it, girl?" Hannah followed the dog's gaze. "Oh."

Remi turned and groaned. "Fox Spinner. What's she doing here?"

"Well, I guess she has time on her hands after leaving me high and dry. I'm sure she'll want to avoid me, too."

On the contrary, Fox waved and came toward them, calling Prima by name. The dog held her ground, growling quietly, as if in solidarity with Hannah's feelings.

Kneeling, Fox gave Prima a good rub and the dog was polite enough to accept it. Then the terrier wedged herself into the small space between Hannah's sneakers.

Hannah stared down, surprised to see a very dark line at the roots of Fox's red hair. She might be a sly Fox in character, but her color was fake.

"Hey," Fox said, getting to her feet. "Sorry I left you in the lurch like that. I got another job and had to start immediately. How are things going?"

"Couldn't be better," Hannah said. "I've added a new manager and a pig this week."

"I heard," Fox said. "Isn't Charlie Garnett a bit old for farming?"

"With age comes wisdom," Hannah said. "He thinks outside the box. Or the paddock." She forced a smile. "I was sorry to lose you, given how close you were to Bob, but I would never want to hold someone back from a great opportunity. What are you doing now?"

"I work in Animal Services," Fox said, slipping a finger under her collar, as if it felt like a noose. "A leadership role."

"I heard you were named assistant director," Remi said. "Must be a dream come true."

"Yeah," Fox said, staring up at the hills. "For sure."

"Then why do you look like you're feeling trapped?" Hannah asked.

"It's an office job, with corporate stupidity," Fox said. "But it's a stepping stone."

"Stepping stone to what?"

Fox offered an enigmatic smile. "The right thing will come up soon. Or so I'm told."

"Well, I wish you the best of luck," Hannah said. "I hope the mayor comes through for you. He's not always reliable."

"I'm good," Fox said. "Don't worry about me."

"I won't," Hannah said. "A fox always lands on its feet."

Fox smirked at this. "You got that right."

"Well, we won't keep you. We're going up, and you're going down."

Fox's eyes narrowed. "Excuse me?"

Hannah gestured to the trail. "I mean, we're still climbing."

"Oh. Okay. I guess I'm a bit sensitive because Cori's been talking smack about me."

Hannah laughed. "Cori talks smack about everyone. Including me."

"For what it's worth, I only left because my job was on the line," Fox said.

"What do you mean?" Hannah asked. "I was happy to have you."

"But you're not calling the shots at Runaway Farm," Fox said. "The mayor is."

"I wouldn't count me out yet," Hannah said.

Fox smirked. "Money doesn't take you as far in Dog Town as you'd think."

"Maybe not, but I'd like to think integrity, a good heart and smart friends can tip the odds in my favor."

"I hope so, too, for the sake of the animals," Fox said. "But I wouldn't bet on it."

Leaning down, Hannah scooped Prima up and started walking. "I wouldn't have bet on Prima and Duncan falling for me either, yet they have. Sometimes you've just got to take a leap of faith."

Heading in the other direction, Fox called back, "Chances are you'll land in a big pile of manure."

"I've smelled worse in Dog Town," Hannah called back. She waved, wishing she had a pair of Cori's trademark gloves.

"Me, too." Remi said. "Check your shoes, Fox."

Fox waved, too, and she didn't need gloves to prove her point.

CHAPTER TEN

I t was no surprise that the hens of Runaway Farm produced generously. Bob had given the mixed flock a handsome rooster, a nice coop and yard, and a variety of nooks and crannies in which to lay. Hannah had quickly grown to enjoy the task of collecting eggs every morning. As soon as there was enough light, she headed out with her basket, greeting the "girls" softly and searching out the little miracles they'd left. It was the one moment in her day when the whole farm notion felt not only believable but achievable.

Three days after the mayor's visit, she'd settled into something of a routine. It had been raining off and on, and now a fragment of a rainbow glimmered in the sky. Gazing up, Hannah made a wish. It seemed ungrateful to ask for more in life but it would also be rash to waste a rainbow.

Charlie was running late because of a flat tire, so she decided to carry on with the morning routine following the itemized list he'd printed, laminated and posted on the wall of the barn. Prima started out at her heels and Hannah appreciated her bristly, tawny shadow. She had never had a dog all her own. Growing up, all the family dogs had pledged strict allegiance to her mother. It felt nice to be a star in her own right.

Prima frisked around and poked into her favorite corners of the barn as Hannah fed and watered the horse, and then scooped pig feed into a bucket. Charlie hadn't been fazed by the prospect of piglets, and said they had over two months to prepare for the impending arrival. That should be plenty of time to get professional builders to add to the outbuildings and fence off more paddocks for pasture. However, half a dozen calls the day before hadn't produced any credible leads. It was strange: even in a city in the throes of development, contractors normally returned calls for smaller jobs.

Heading out to Wilma's pen, she saw the pig nosing around what appeared to be a pile of rocks on the far side of the large pen. She called her, and then banged the pail against the fence, a sound that normally brought the sow at a brisk trot. This time, she didn't even raise her head.

"What's she eating?" Hannah said to Prima. She opened the gate and the dog slipped through ahead of her. Crossing the muddy pen, she saw a mound of green acorns. There were no oak trees anywhere near the barn; even if there had been, there was no way they'd fall into a concentrated pile like that. There were hundreds of them, and no telling how many the pig had already eaten.

"That's enough," she said, moving her new work boots under the pig's snout. She stepped over the acorns to fend her off, but the pig was equally determined to get them. "No," she said. "Leave it."

Cori had said that pigs were as bright as dogs, but Wilma hadn't gone through basic obedience. She refused to back off, and Hannah became more insistent, trying to shove the 500 pound animal aside.

Prima joined the effort, nipping at Wilma's legs. The pig finally moved away, giving a shrill, frustrated squeal. Emboldened, Prima herded her even further across the pen, barking.

Kneeling in the muck, Hannah scraped the acorns together with her hands and hurled handfuls over the fence. She had no idea if acorns were harmful for pigs, but they weren't on Charlie's extensive list of approved pig food.

Approved or not, the hungry pig wanted the nuts. She tried to deke around the nipping dog and circle back.

"Prima, come," Hannah said, worried the dog would get trampled if Wilma became irate. Although the dog didn't fully comply, she fell back and settled for zooming in short bursts between Hannah and the pig.

Wilma stood still, snorting. It looked as if she had given up. Hannah kept an eye on her, gathering the last of the acorns. As she picked them up, one by one, Wilma gave another sudden squeal and began running toward her. There was no time to move out of the way. Hannah threw the acorns down as decoy, hoping Wilma would slow her roll. On the contrary, the pig picked up speed, her squeal rising to a painful pitch matched only by Prima's furious barking. The dog ran alongside the pig, leaping at her, and then finally grabbed the pig's ear.

Wilma shook her off easily, and continued. For a large animal, she could move surprisingly quickly. In what seemed like seconds, the pink damp snout, a dirt-encrusted disk, collided with Hannah's forehead, and she flipped over onto her back. She waited for worse to follow, but Wilma moved aside and started snuffling for the last of the acorns. Prima stood between them, growling.

Lying in the mud, surrounded by pig manure, Hannah stared up at the sky. The rainbow had vanished and reality set in. She'd have to be more careful. It was one thing to be cavalier with her own safety, but for the moment at least, there was another life on board. The doctor had reminded her that more than 30 percent of conceptions miscarried early, and Hannah suspected that might very well happen. It had all been too easy. She'd been told the process would likely take months—months in which she could change her mind. But Mother Nature had been surprisingly agreeable about shaking hands with medical technology.

Finally she clambered to her feet. She was none the worse for her tumble, other than stinking. Whether Wilma had deliberately spared her, or been decoyed by the acorns, she wasn't sure. The pig hoovered up the remaining nuts, and then stared at Hannah with beady eyes.

Warning eyes.

The pig was between Hannah and the gate. Discretion seemed like the better plan. If she ran to the other end of the pen, she could scale the fence near the driveway.

No sooner had the idea formed in her mind than Wilma began heading in the same direction. Had she given away her plan with a gesture, or was the pig more intuitive than she expected?

Well, she could still outrun a pig, of that much she was sure. "Prima, come," she called, as she started clomping through puddles in heavy work boots. The dog was hard on her heels, and the pig was gaining on them. It was slow going in the slippery mud.

Reaching the fence, she leaned and scooped up the terrier. She propped one foot on the lower rung of the fence and hoisted herself up with her free hand. Leaning over, she lowered the dog over the other side and dropped her to safety. Then she swung one leg over, swaying as Wilma grabbed the rolled-up cuff of her overalls and pulled.

Shaking her leg, she tried to free her pants without booting the pig. Aggressive as Wilma might be, she was just a rescued animal, and a pregnant one at that. Hormones probably made the pig cranky. At the moment, Hannah knew exactly how that felt. Anger flared in her roiling belly and she shouted, "Get off me, you ungrateful pig."

"Hannah!" There was a shout from behind her, but she didn't turn. She was clinging to the top rung as if it were a bucking bronco. One wrong move and she could be tossed.

Suddenly there were hands around her waist. Big, strong, assured hands. Letting go, she allowed herself to drop into someone's arms.

"Thank you, thank you," she said. She leaned back and looked up into Nick Springdale's handsome face.

Nick spun around, still cradling her. "Are you okay?" He set her on her feet and held her steady, while his golden retriever, Clive, did a little dance of greeting with Prima. The bigger dog was a little standoffish, which put Prima at ease. She didn't appreciate dogs who took liberties, like Leo.

"Yes, fine." Hannah mentally scanned herself from head to foot. She *was* fine, if a little shaken up. "Wilma and I had a disagreement over her breakfast, that's all."

"Did she win?" he asked.

His hand was still on her arm and she moved away, reminding herself that a few nights ago, he'd won a stuffed animal for a blonde woman at the fair. It wasn't that he owed her anything. Far from it. But the fact she was so quickly and easily replaced showed his interest was never genuine in the first place.

Grabbing her phone, she tapped with both thumbs and then shook her head. "Looks like we both lose. Wilma ate green acorns, and they're toxic to pigs. I'll need to call the vet."

Nick stared over her shoulder. "I don't see any oak trees. How did acorns end up in her pen? And in spring, yet?"

Heading for the house, Hannah quickly pressed the vet's number. A month ago, she hadn't known there was such a thing as an agrarian vet who made house calls for farm animals. Now, she'd used the number so often she'd committed it to memory.

"I can't imagine where the acorns came from," she told Nick. "They weren't there last evening. Maybe someone was trying to be nice."

"Trespassing on your property overnight?"

"Apparently." On the porch, she paused and left a breathless voicemail for the vet. "I'm sure he'll call me back soon. Do you want to come in? I need to change."

He held the door and she noticed he gave her a wide berth. She must really stink.

"Hey!" Nick's hand shot up just in time to shield his face from Duncan.

"Sorry," she said, offering her arm to the parrot. "He's getting possessive of me, I think." They'd made such progress that Duncan preferred to ride around with her when she was inside the house, only returning to his perch to eat or do his business. When his feathers settled, she said, "You can pat him now, if you like."

"No thanks," Nick said. "I'm not a big fan of birds. Or anything but dogs, really."

"Oh, right." Hannah smiled. "Evie told me you two weren't raised with pets and are easily spooked."

He straightened his broad shoulders. "I wouldn't say spooked. I just prefer predictable animals. Parrots aren't predictable."

"Until you get to know them. All it takes is a little patience." She walked towards Duncan's perch in the corner. "I assume it'll be the same with the pig."

The bird hopped off when they passed the recliner and fluttered into the seat.

"He's torn up the upholstery," Nick said.

She nodded. "I think he's building a nest."

"A nest? Isn't Duncan a male?"

"So I was told," she said. "'One African gray male. Handsome. Protective. Profane. Seeking wife.'"

Nick held tight to Clive's leash. The dog was more curious about the bird than about Prima.

"Maybe you're the prospective bride," he said. "I think he's looking at you funny."

"I've already told him it'll never work. And he told me to shut up."

Nick gave a barky laugh that was oddly charming. It made Hannah smile, and then try to erase the smile. She looked down at her baggy, soiled overalls. These would come in handy when she started to show. For now, there was no reason to tell Nick or anyone else about her current condition. Remi was the only one who knew the truth. Charlie obviously suspected but hadn't asked for confirmation. If and when it became necessary to tell people, she could figure out appropriate messaging.

"I guess I'm the first one here," Nick said, after a long pause.

"First one?"

"Remi called to say you needed a hand with some repairs. Tiller, Sullivan and Carver Black are coming as well."

"That's wonderful, but you didn't need to. I've made some calls."

Nick sighed. "I'm afraid you won't get the response you want. Carver is well connected in contracting, and he says you've been blacklisted."

"Blacklisted! Why?"

Now Nick looked down. "Carver can explain better than I can, probably."

Hannah sighed. "Mayor Bradshaw strikes again, I assume. He's warning everyone off Runaway Farm."

"Not everyone. He's more discreet than that. But probably everyone good."

Duncan got tired of waiting and uttered a string of profanity.

"I couldn't agree more," she said.

Nick laughed. "Don't worry. You'll have plenty of help. I may not be able to fly you to the tropics, like Duncan, but I'm probably better with a hammer."

"I appreciate the help, but I have major projects ahead. Are you saying no skilled professional will work for me?"

"Only from Dorset Hills," Nick said. "There are other counties. Don't worry."

She shook her head. "It sounds like the mayor is willing to put my farm and even my animals' welfare at risk. There's cause for worry."

"This stuff always simmers down," Nick said. "I'll ask Evie how to handle the politics."

"Don't bother her," Hannah said. "I'll figure something out."

Her phone rang, and after a few moments of conversation with the vet she hung up. "First, I'll give Cori a call to see if she can figure out who's trying to poison my pig."

CHAPTER ELEVEN

After Charlie and the other men arrived, they toured the property to make a list of the most pressing needs for repair. Hannah's bigger plans for renovating the house would need to be postponed until the mayor's arm could be twisted hard enough to get the necessary permits.

"Don't get discouraged," Nick said, as she walked him to the car. "The mayor always gives in eventually."

That's not how Hannah remembered it. In every story of triumph over Bill Bradshaw, he had been cornered and threatened in some way. His recent spiritual renewal certainly hadn't brought about a full transformation. But she didn't want to be negative with Nick, who was definitely a glass-half-full sort of guy. She liked that in a man. Even if she couldn't allow herself to like the man in the way she might have before the time of Runaway Farm, vicious pigs and expanding families.

"Of course," Hannah said. "It's just tiring, trying to outmaneuver the man in charge—especially if he's condoning someone trying to harm my livestock."

Leaning on his truck, Nick shook his head. "I've known

Bill Bradshaw for years. He's no sweetheart, but I don't think he'd deliberately harm any animal. At the very least, it could hurt the town's brand."

"I hope you're right. Normally when someone goes low, I go high. When there's an animal involved, however, I'll go as low—and as far—as I need to."

"Speaking of which... how about I give you a driving lesson? It's a nice day for it."

"Uh, now?" She ran her hands over her hoodie and jeans. Her clothes might be fresh, but she knew the scent of pig manure still clung to her. In the confines of a vehicle, it would be gag-inducing.

"No time like the present," he said. "You shouldn't be stuck out here without wheels, Hannah."

"Good thing I got myself some wheels, then." With a sheepish grin, she led him to the garage beside the barn. Rolling up the door with as much of a flourish as the creaky old thing would allow, she waved her arm. "Voila. Wheels."

Inside sat a pristine golf cart. It was white, with a neon orange stripe along the side that reminded her of Cori's gloves.

Nick's laugh started out barky and ripened to a low roll. It was impossible not to join him, even when a crusty lock of her own hair fell into her face, reminding her of how much life had changed recently.

"You're not going to drive that on the highway, I hope," he said.

"According to Sally Taylor, it's safe on the shoulder or on the better trails. This baby goes over 20 miles per hour."

"That doesn't sound like a great idea, Hannah."

"That's because you haven't had an omelet made with Runaway Farm eggs," she said, lifting the lid of a cooler in the back seat. Six dozen eggs sat inside, waiting for delivery. "Gotta motor, Nick. People are waiting."

Shaking his head, he climbed into the truck and followed her out to the main road. He turned left and headed into town; she turned right and drove along the shoulder, careful to miss the most obvious bumps to preserve her precious cargo.

The first stop was Sally's house. The property was immaculate and the home unexpectedly beautiful. It was a large, rustic cottage with a cathedral-style ceiling and glass all the way up one side. Hannah hadn't seen anything like it in Dorset Hills.

She pressed the horn and the cart gave a nasal honk. It was enough to bring Sally out onto the porch with a little white bichon cross under her arm. She came down the stairs, laughing. "Hannah Pemberton, I underestimated you."

"That happens a lot," Hannah said. "But I credit you for this idea." Slapping the side of the golf cart, she hopped out and collected a dozen eggs. "I'm happy to carry on Bob's tradition."

Sally beckoned. "Come inside for a coffee." In the front hall, she sniffed. "No offense dear, but you brought the farm with you."

Hannah told her about the encounter with Wilma that morning. "The vet said even a bushel of acorns wouldn't be enough to harm her, luckily. But I have to assume someone had ill intent."

"Where would someone even get acorns at this time of year?" Sally asked, plugging in the kettle. "It must have been one of the mayor's cronies."

"Who else would wish harm on a rescue pig?" Hannah sat down at the kitchen table and looked around. The kitchen was bright, welcoming and spotless. No wonder Sally had been so meticulous around Runaway Farm. She hadn't really been needed since Charlie came on board, however. He had the place whipped into shape already.

"How about the pig's former owner?" Sally asked. "I heard he was pretty burned about whatever it is you said to him."

"I overpaid him. Plus I saved him fines for not reporting him to Animal Services. Wilma's a hundred pounds underweight and has two skin conditions. Her vet care will cost close to a grand."

"I know all that," Sally reminded her gently, as she poured hot water over ground coffee in a drip cone. "I'm just pointing out another possible suspect. I've known Bill Bradshaw for years, and while he always had an ego, I just don't think he has it in him to hurt an animal deliberately."

"He's sent good dogs to other counties. Taken them away from loving families to dubious futures. That sounds like hurting an animal to me."

Sally joined her at the table. "Don't get me wrong, Hannah. I don't agree with much Bill's done since he came into office. But I do think *he* believes he's putting this town first. No matter how silly some of his policies look."

Hannah sipped her coffee and set it down. She used to love a strong cup of black coffee, but for the past six weeks, it had been giving her heartburn. At least now she knew why.

"Did Bob Hess have other enemies?" she asked. "Anyone who'd carry out a grudge?"

Sally gazed at Hannah with warm brown eyes. "Probably. Like anyone in animal rescue, Bob had adversaries. Charlie does, too, although he kept a lower profile as he rose up the ranks at his job. He's not squeaky clean, and Bob wasn't either."

"Charlie said he used to bend the law."

"Bob did more than bend it. And people have very long memories. Cori can tell you that."

"Oh, yes. She's Dog Town's most wanted."

Pushing the cream and sugar across the table, Sally said, "And then there's Bob's family. His nephews were incensed about him selling to you before he passed. They thought he'd lost his faculties."

"I paid him well, but he bequeathed his entire estate to animal charities," Hannah said. "The mayor himself told me Bob's nephews backed selling to developers, so yes, I suppose their noses are out of joint. But anyone who met Bob even once knew he'd put animals first. That was his mission in life."

Sally nudged the creamer over a little more. "Coffee okay?"

"It's great, thanks." Hannah took a mouthful and felt the hot liquid searing her esophagus all the way down. "What do you think I should do?"

"As Bob's friend, I'd tell you to fight the good fight. Get Cori on board and do what she tells you." She added a spoonful of sugar to her coffee and stirred vigorously, clinking against the mug. "As *your* new friend, I'd recommend a softer stance. Do you want to be constantly at odds with the City?"

Hannah shook her head. "I promised Bob and I keep my word."

"I admire you for that, I really do," Sally said. "But look what happened with Wilma. Bob would never want an animal harmed for the sake of making a point to the City."

Eyes fixed on the dark brew in her cup, Hannah sighed. "You've got a point there."

Reaching across the table, Sally squeezed her forearm. "You're taking all this too hard. You look so pale."

"I'm okay." Her voice shook a little. Sally's kindness was motherly enough to stir the old embers of grief that would probably never go out. She didn't even want them to go out, for fear of forgetting her mom.

"You're pushing yourself too much," Sally said. "Maybe you need some time alone to think about all of this."

Pushing her chair back, Hannah rose abruptly. "Maybe. Then I guess I'd better finish my deliveries and get home." Walking out ahead of Sally, she looked into the living room, with its soaring ceiling. "You have a beautiful home, Sally. You must be happy here."

"Very." She picked up her bichon and cuddled him. "Although I think Snowball would like living in town."

Running down the stairs to the golf cart, Hannah called, "He'd be bored in 10 minutes. City life isn't all it's cracked up to be."

"Egg pun," Sally called back. "That's the spirit."

Hannah pressed the pedal to the floor. "Right? I crack me up."

HANNAH CAREERED down her driveway towards the house, swerving around potholes like a pro. She slowed when she saw half a dozen vehicles in the parking area. All the usual suspects were waiting on the porch in the magic hour before sunset. When she pulled up, there was a round of applause.

Hopping out, she gave an elaborate bow, patting Prima

on the way by. "Today a golf cart, tomorrow an all-terrain vehicle."

"Or you could just get a truck, like a normal person," Cori said, from her perch on the upper step.

"I'm not normal," Hannah said. "Is that why I didn't get an invitation to my own party?"

"It's a strategy meeting," Cori said. "I heard about the attack on Wilma. From Sally. And from Remi via Nick. It's the type of thing I'd expect to hear directly from you."

Hannah sighed as she sat sideways on the stair below Cori's. "I intended to call you after coming up with my own strategy while I was delivering eggs. But every single person invited me in for coffee or tea and time got away on me."

Remi set Leo down and he made a beeline for Hannah. He instinctively knew who needed him most in any crowd. Prima lifted her lip at the beagle. He might be the best therapy dog, but she'd claimed Hannah for her very own now.

"Did anyone have theories?" Cori asked, watching Leo and Prima as they vied for Hannah's attention.

"Bob's relatives and old enemies rose to the top of the heap as pig-poisoning suspects," Hannah said, pulling Prima into her lap, and kissing Leo on the head. "But Fox Spinner was a close second and some even threw shade on Charlie."

Cori's mouth puckered. "I've known Fox and Charlie for a decade and vouch for them both personally. Strike them from your list, because, as we've established, I'm never wrong."

"Just a distraction from the real culprit," Duff said, from her lawn chair on the porch. "This has the mayor's name written all over it."

"Maybe," Bridget said, bravely swinging her legs from

the rickety railing. "I'm not convinced. I've seen his work, and this is just too... obvious."

"I don't feel great about leaving the goats here overnight," Cori said.

"Goats?" Hannah said. "What goats?"

"Just a couple of kids I rescued," Cori said. "Quite the characters."

"You ran it by Charlie?" Hannah asked. "He says you can't just throw any animals together."

"They're in the last shed, so it's all good. I'll pick them up tomorrow."

"Can you give me a few pointers about handling Wilma while you're here? She's feral."

"She's a typical pregnant sow. You stole her food."

"Where would someone find acorns at this time of year?"

Cori shrugged. "You can get crazy things online these days. I do."

Remi came down the stairs to stand in front of them. "Big picture, ladies. Regardless of what happened with Wilma, we need a plan for turning the mayor in our favor."

Cori waved one gloved hand, as if swatting an annoying fly. "No problem. I have an idea."

CHAPTER TWELVE

"I hate this idea," Hannah said, hugging herself with folded arms as a dozen vehicles jockeyed for position in the gravel parking area outside her barn. Even more were turning in from the highway.

"Don't worry, it's going to be great," Remi said, transferring Leo from one arm to the other. The fact that his paws hadn't touched down for an hour told Hannah that Remi wasn't as confident about that as she sounded.

Someone leaned out of a truck and yelled, "Yeehaw!"

"Who even does that?" Hannah asked. "I didn't realize we have yokels in Dorset Hills."

"Community events like this bring out the best and the worst in people," Remi said. "We've found it's the fastest way to get the mayor's attention. When the masses speak, he listens."

"Here I was thinking money talked," Hannah said. "Seems like it falls on deaf ears in Dog Town."

"Oh, money talks. It's just that developer dollars speak louder than yours," Remi said, grinning. "They put all their wallets together and shouted you down. That's all the mayor hears right now."

Bridget, Duff, Sasha, Ari and Flynn Strathmore were guiding people into parking spaces and serving as official greeters. Mim handed every child a brightly colored map created by Flynn and a bag of equally bright fruit and vegetables. Meanwhile Charlie, Cori, Maisie, Nika and Sally Taylor were at their posts with the various animals.

Cori's idea to open Runaway Farm to the public as a petting zoo on Saturdays had caught on like wildfire. With very little promotion, word had gotten around and families arrived in droves. This was the only site within 50 miles of City Hall that children could offer carrots to baby goats and lambs, collect eggs from hens, pat sweet heifers, and take slow rides around a new paddock on a calm old mare. Only Wilma, in her new pen built by Nick, Carver, Tiller and Sullivan, was strictly hands-off. Cori had studied her over the past few days, and decreed the pig too much of a wild card to be included in the merriment. However, the kids could drop apples and carrots into the pen, under Sally's supervision. Wilma showed little interest in their offerings. Although she'd survived the acorn incident with no more than a minor bellyache, her appetite was still a bit off.

Hannah ruled the house off-limits as well. They'd set up tables outside with free lemonade and cookies for the kids, and urns of hot tea and coffee for the adults. As it turned out, many of the guests had brought coolers with more exotic beverages. One couple was staggering around intoxicated, with Maisie keeping a close eye on them.

Shaking her head, Remi said, "Two bad apples spoil things for everyone. Cori's going to use the gloves on them before the morning's out, mark my words."

"Sometimes I wonder if she comes up with these ideas

just to have an excuse to teach people lessons," Hannah said. "Maybe we should go and run interference."

Putting Prima inside the house, she locked the door. The little terrier was almost as crusty with strangers as Wilma the pig so it was better this way. Several visitors had ignored the "No Dogs" rule, and since the May day was too warm to leave pets in vehicles, the dogs circulated, leashed, with their owners.

Hannah and Remi stopped first at the largest paddock, where Charlie was leading Florence around with child after child on board.

"All good, Charlie?" Hannah called.

He tipped his cowboy hat and smiled. Cori's schemes weren't new to him and he pretty much went with the flow.

Maisie, the tall dog groomer with wild blonde corkscrew curls, was enduring worse at her station. Two adorable brown baby goats with green eyes and horizontal pupils ping-ponged around their enclosure. The little clowns never stopped moving, bouncing off each other—and Maisie—in an endless show. However, they were so entranced with each other that they didn't cater to the audience. The row of people along the fence started complaining when the goats refused to come over to be fed.

"What's the point of a petting zoo if the animals won't actually let you pet them?" said a man in a Batman shirt.

"Total rip-off," another man said. "I won't be coming back here."

Normally diplomatic, Remi took umbrage today. "The event is free," she said. "You can't get this close to goats, sheep or cows anywhere else in Dog Town."

"Waste of time," Batman said. "You can see funnier goats on social media."

"Exactly," the other man agreed. "From the comfort of

your own recliner. I came here so my kids could pet animals, and feed them."

"You can pet the horse," Hannah said. "And really, it's safest for everyone if there's a respectful distance. Animals are unpredictable."

"You're just worried about being sued if someone gets hurt," Batman said. "As if you couldn't afford insurance."

"I have insurance," Hannah said. "I'm sorry you're not enjoying your visit. I guess watching sweet animals up close isn't for everyone. But it fills my heart with joy every day."

The two men went back to complaining about the goats and she moved on to another large paddock, which currently held the sheep. Cori had brought along Clem, her black and white border collie, and was demonstrating herding techniques for a couple of dozen people. The dog hustled the sheep around the pen in various formations, following Cori's hand gestures and whistles, and finally drove them back into their shelter in the corner. This audience was decidedly more appreciative, and applauded when Clem returned to Cori's side.

A little girl looked up at her mom and said, "Can we come back next week?"

The mother looked at Hannah. "Will you be open every weekend?"

"I'm not sure yet," Hannah said. "Probably not."

The little girl promptly burst into tears. "But I wanna ride Florence again."

"You can ride Florence again, I promise," Hannah said.

The mother gave Hannah a weary smile as she hoisted the little girl to her hip and walked away. "Don't make promises to kids that you can't keep. Recipe for disaster."

Following slowly, Hannah muttered, "I'll make a terrible mom."

Remi stopped walking and turned. "Don't even say that. It's not like you just know these things automatically. Parents learn by doing."

"I made that little girl cry."

"She's just overexcited and tired. And when you open the farm to visitors again, they'll be the first ones here."

They headed around the back of the barn, picking their way over rougher terrain. "I don't know if I can do this again, Remi. I value my privacy too much. We may need to find another way to turn the tide against—"

The last words died in her throat as they came around to Wilma's pen. The drunk couple was inside the pen with the pig, and Sally was nowhere to be seen. The woman flourished her red jacket in the pig's general direction, while the man circled around behind Wilma. The pig watched them both with small pinkish eyes. She almost seemed made of stone, but then her ears flickered.

"Hey!" Hannah called. "Get out of there now, you two."

"Please," Remi called. "The pig is very anxious. She's just come out of a bad situation."

Ignoring them, the man poked Wilma in the backside with a broom handle. That was enough to bring Wilma back to life. She started trotting towards the woman, who just laughed and waved her coat around a little more.

"Wilma, no!" Hannah called. The gate was too far away, so she started climbing the fence. "Come!"

Remi climbed after her and headed for the man, who was now staggering toward his wife yelling, "Stop, you pig!"

The pig picked up speed, now charging. The drunk woman clumsily dodged out of the way, tripped over her own jacket and fell into the muck. Wilma tried at the last minute to dodge around her, missed and jumped over her legs. Squeals and shrieks overlapped, and people came running.

Hannah reached the woman first, pulling her to her feet. Cori had seemingly catapulted into the pen and carried a pole with a hook on the end.

The tool wasn't necessary. Wilma simply stood beside the woman, as if she'd turned to stone again.

"She bit me," the woman said, leaning against her husband, who could barely hold her upright.

There was a small gash on the woman's leg where the pig had grazed her.

"This pig did not bite you," Hannah said. "She touched you with her hoof when she jumped to avoid you."

"She bit her. I saw it all," the man slurred.

"We saw it all, too," Hannah said. "Did you see the huge sign that says, 'Do not enter'?"

"What sign?" he asked.

Hannah turned to point it out and noticed the sign was missing. She also saw a familiar figure walking away. A woman in baggy overalls, with a long red ponytail. Fox Spinner. She had a small child clinging to her hand.

"What's Fox doing here?" Remi whispered.

"Spying for the mayor, probably," Hannah said. "Do you think she took down the sign?"

Remi shook her head. "Fox wouldn't care if these people got turned into pig feed. But she *would* care if Wilma got indigestion."

Hannah laughed, tried to supress it, and then giggled harder.

"You think this is funny?" the drunk man said. "My wife could have died."

He tried to lead the woman away but she dragged

behind, yelling, "I'll shue your rich ash, Hannah Pembershun."

Cori raised the hook and Remi said, "Cori, don't."

"Don't what? I'm just pointing the way out."

The drunk couple tried to climb the fence and failed. Remi walked over, guided them to the gate, and opened it. Then she snapped her fingers for Leo and escorted the couple to their car.

"Where's Sally?" Cori asked. "She was on pig patrol. This shouldn't have happened."

Leaving Nika to guard Wilma's pen, they circled the house to find Sally on the front porch arguing with the guy in the Batman T-shirt. Still carrying the hook, Cori raced up the stairs like a tiny gladiator.

"This guy got into the house somehow," Sally said. "I was with the pig when I heard Duncan screeching bloody murder. I caught the guy coming outside with the parrot."

"I just wanted my kid to see the bird," Batman said. "I saw the parrot sitting in the window and figured that, at least, was worth coming out for."

"You were leaving the house with an uncaged bird," Cori said. "That sounds like birdnapping."

"A locked house," Hannah said. "That sounds like breaking and entering."

Batman shrugged. "The bathroom window was unlocked."

"Call the cops," Cori said, advancing on Batman.

"Don't," he said, and his tone changed instantly. "I didn't mean the bird any harm. I thought he would stay on my arm."

That was when Hannah realized. "Where is he? Where's my parrot?"

"Flew into the tree," Batman said, pointing to a huge maple beside the porch.

Hannah turned and looked up. "Duncan? Duncan!"

There was a gray swoosh as the bird dropped from the tree and landed on her shoulder. "Oh, thank goodness," she said. "You're safe."

"Pretty lassie," the bird croaked, nibbling her ear gently.

In the parking area, Fox gave a honk and a wave as she drove off.

"Is that a new truck?" Cori said. "Fancy."

"Wonder how she bought *that* on a government wage?" Remi asked. "Maybe she had some help."

Hannah cleared her throat and nodded at Batman, who was still blocked on the porch by Cori's hooked pole.

"Right," Cori said, moving away from the man. "You are so lucky that parrot came back, buddy."

"I'm sure the dog hasn't gone far, either," he said. "But she ran like a bat out of hell."

Handing the parrot to Cori, Hannah rushed down the steps in a panic, only to see a dog-sized tornado whirling up the driveway. The dusty dog took a leap and hit Hannah square in the chest.

"This place is going to be the death of me," she said, hugging the terrier. "One way or another."

CHAPTER THIRTEEN

Aladdin the rooster woke Hannah as usual the next day. It was a sound she'd unexpectedly grown to love because it signaled the start of the brief time she could count on being alone at Runaway Farm. Her fears of being isolated on the outskirts had so far proven completely unfounded. Aside from Charlie's company, she had various friends coming and going, and now tradesmen were coming from other counties, making their pitches for the renovations she needed. When she lived in New York, she'd been surrounded by people and often felt lonely. Here, she was never lonely but sometimes craved solitude. In the beautiful hour at dawn, it was just her.

Well, just her, over 40 chickens and the rest of the menagerie.

Best of all, there was her constant companion, Prima, the territorial terrier. The dog, like the parrot, had become quite possessive of her and didn't go far, even if she was released by hooligans. Hannah wondered if she gave off a damsel in distress vibe that animals could detect. The parrot Casanova was a bit much, with his grooming of her hair, croaky endearments and nest-building. But Prima had quickly convinced her that no one owned by a dog is ever really lonely.

Heading for the henhouse, she wondered if she'd have ever embarked on Project Motherhood if she'd paired up with a good dog first. There were other reasons—good ones —that she'd made her decision. Loneliness wasn't on her list but perhaps it had been an unconscious factor propelling her forward.

Well, there was no point second-guessing now. That particular horse had left the barn. As long as things went as she hoped they would, she would have her child and soli-tude would continue to be a rare gift for the next 20 years.

"Good morning, ladies," she called, strolling in among the chickens. The smell of bird poop used to bother her— even make her queasy—but once she got the hang of mouth-breathing, that faded. In fact, mouth breathing was her greatest ally here on the farm. She just hoped she'd remember to use her nose in polite company.

Stretching egg collection as long as she could, she listened for Charlie's truck. If he hadn't arrived by the time she was done with the hens, she felt obliged to start the grunt work with the other livestock. It was hard to relax knowing they were all waiting and hungry.

Wilma, with her growing load of piglets, was first up. After scooping pig pellets and vegetables into a pail, she headed around the side of the barn.

"Wilma," she called. "Come." She had listened to Cori's instructions on winning over the pig. First and fore-most was making her work for her food. Cori called it the Nothing in Life is Free approach, and it was apparently just as useful for pigs as dogs. Wilma needed to learn that Hannah was the woman behind the food bucket, and as such deserving of respect. Only then would she stop menacing her when she was in the pen. Until that happened, Hannah had promised Remi she wouldn't go into the pen at all.

Since learning Hannah's news, Remi had been sticking even closer, her face a mask of guilt over roping Hannah into buying the farm. All Hannah could do was continue to reassure her friend that she had no regrets, despite the changed circumstances. As challenging as the current situation was, she had no desire to return to her pristine apartment in New York. Runaway Farm might be the death of her, but it had also brought her new life.

When she rounded the corner, she saw Wilma had refused to come when called. This pig was stubborn. Hungry as she was, she continued to thumb her nose at authority.

"Wilma, come!" she called again, peering around the large enclosure and finding no sign of her. There was a child's wading pool at one end, near her mud wallow, various toys to keep a porcine mind challenged, and a newly built shelter for shade. But nothing could hide a 500-pound pig from view. Just the same, she set down the pail and ran around the circumference of the yard to be sure.

There was no sign of Wilma.

Neither was there a sign of a breach anywhere. Coming around to the gate, her heart dropped into her work boots. The long metal chain that had been wrapped around the fencepost now lay on the ground. Beside it, the padlock was snapped neatly in two.

"RELAX," Cori said, leading the Mafia through the mile of

bush that separated Hannah's home from Sally Taylor's. "Pigs are natural foragers. She'll be fine."

"She's pregnant," Remi said. "She needs care."

"Pregnant doesn't mean medically fragile," Cori said. "She's spent most of her life pregnant and she's still fighting, isn't she?"

"I'm more concerned about how she got out," Hannah said.

Looking over her shoulder, Cori blew long bangs out of her dark eyes. "Isn't that obvious? Someone's messing with you."

"That much is obvious, yes. But who? And why?"

Cori shook her head. "Duh. What rhymes with 'pill' and rules the town?"

Catching up with her, Hannah said, "Why would Bill Bradshaw stoop so low as to set a pig free?"

"He didn't do it himself, I'm sure," Cori said. "One of his many dedicated followers would have lifted the latch so he didn't break a nail."

"But still, it seems petty even for Bill," Hannah said.

"You know you're the only one of us who calls him Bill, right?" Cori made sure her orange fingers were visible as she brushed back her hair. "Do you really want to stay on a first-name basis with Mayor Bradshaw now?"

"If his henchmen are stealing my animals, then I guess he's just a plain old 'mayor' to me."

Holding a branch back so that the others could follow, Cori said, "I'd go with something stronger."

"I still don't get what he has to gain from setting my pig loose. What am I missing?"

"Think like Bill the Pill," Bridget said, grinning. "Be strategic and also slimy. I know it's hard to put yourself in that mindset, but you can do it."

Bridget's hand rested on Beau's head, as it almost always did. It was like she was tuning into his knowledge, somehow. Inevitably, she ended up in the lead, and unlike the others, she rarely stumbled on rocks or got swatted by branches.

Hannah pondered for a moment. "Okay. So, if my animals are running loose, it makes me look bad to the community, right? Irresponsible."

"Good," Bridget said. "What else?"

"It's a *pregnant* pig," Sasha chimed in. "When my dog was pregnant, it reflected very poorly on me. Bringing unsanctioned life into this town is frowned upon."

Remi glanced over at Hannah and pressed her lips together. Silently, she lifted Leo and tried handing him to Hannah.

"Don't carry that beagle," Cori snapped. "Either of you. You need your hands free to deflect."

Leo's tail continued to wag steadily when his paws hit the earth again. Up, down and all around... it was all in a day's work for the town's most popular therapy beagle. Hannah had wanted to bring Prima along, but feared she'd take off to hunt squirrels. The dog was reasonably obedient, but Cori had cautioned her about the terrier's high prey drive. Losing one animal that day was hard enough.

"She's a belligerent pig," Bridget suggested. "The mayor wouldn't like that."

"He most certainly would not," Duff said. As the only one in heels, she struggled to keep up, but she managed. It was clearly a point of pride. "An aggressive pig is worse than an aggressive dog. Zero tolerance."

"She's not aggressive," Hannah said. "Just grouchy. She only nipped me once."

Cori held an index finger to her lips, letting the middle

one come along for the ride. "I'd keep the part about biting to yourself, Hannah. That would make Wilma a threat to public safety."

"A dangerous pig is bacon," Maisie said. Her bright smile didn't fade in the slightest. She was the most matter-of-fact of the Rescue Mafia. When Cori got worked up, and Bridget simmered into silence, Maisie just carried on, imminently practical. She didn't get enough credit, Hannah thought, mostly because she didn't ask for it.

After walking quietly for a while, Hannah spoke again. "So you think Mayor Bradshaw is setting me up. The word gets around that my dangerous pig is running amok and it looks bad for Runaway Farm."

"Bingo," Cori said.

Duff grabbed a tree for balance. "I predict some bogus sightings. Reports of backyard invasions."

"Better yet, leaked photos," Maisie said. "Where Wilma looks muddy and crazed."

"She'll look crazed for real, because she's hungry," Remi said. "Poor thing. She'll tip trash cans and chew up gardens. Dorset Hills doesn't like a mess."

"One day someone will corner her in a yard and she'll knock them over trying to escape," Duff said. "If the mayor plays his cards right, it'll be a little old lady who can wave from a hospital bed for the cameras."

"Your face will hit the front pages as the owner of the feral pig terrorizing the good people of Dog Town," Bridget said.

"His techniques are becoming predictable," Remi said, sighing.

"If he's becoming predicable, then we can outthink him," Hannah said. "How hard can it be?"

"It's hard for normal people like us to stoop as low as he does," Duff said. "But not impossible."

"It's not a stretch for me at all," Cori said. "The only problem is that he has a fleet of sneaky staff, so we have to be nimble."

"Including Fox Spinner," Hannah reminded her.

"I still vouch for Fox," Cori said. "But I'm doing my due diligence, trust me."

Hannah looked around at the crew. Every one of the women looked animated, as if the challenge energized them. Their mood was infectious.

"If he thinks I'm going down over a lost pig, he's wrong," she said. "Bill Bradshaw will need to bring his A game because I've got something he doesn't."

"Money doesn't take you as far in Dog Town as you might think," Cori said. "That's why I keep telling you not to rest on your dollar signs."

"It's not my money he needs to worry about," Hannah said, as they finally broke free of the bush and staggered into Sally Taylor's yard. "It's cognitive capital."

Brushing dirt from her jeans, from a spill, Remi asked, "Is that big city code?"

Hannah laughed. "It's a small-town tribute to a bunch of smart friends. With you guys on my side, Bill the Pill's got his work cut out for him."

Cori held up her gloved hand and gave Hannah a rare high five. "May this pig be the thing that finally crushes Bill Bradshaw."

CHAPTER FOURTEEN

Aladdin's alarm services weren't needed after Wilma's disappearance. The past three mornings Hannah had catapulted out of bed at the crack of dawn to continue the search. The group had swelled the second day with the extended Mafia, including Sally, Charlie and the rest of the men. There didn't seem to be a stone left unturned for miles, but somehow a 500-pound pig managed to stay concealed. Hannah began wondering if Wilma had not just been set free, but pignapped. Given the difficulty of transporting the pig to the farm, however, she was hard pressed to believe she could have slept through an abduction. Wilma was far too stubborn to just hop into someone's truck and go for a ride.

The day before, Hannah had covered miles with Remi, pinning LOST posters to poles. Later in the day, Bridget had sent photos of the same poles, now bare. Someone had torn down the posters. This morning, after chores, she would put them all back up again. Then, she'd circulate in her golf cart all day, trying to catch the perpetrator.

Whoever removed the signs must be in the mayor's back pocket, and may have had a hand in freeing her pig.

On top of that, she'd offer a big reward. Really big. So ridiculously big that even the mayor's henchmen would be tortured in turning it down. The mayor would have to bribe them in obvious ways for their sacrifice. Fox Spinner had been rewarded with a job and possibly a new truck, but she still wasn't satisfied. She was holding out for something better, and maybe the pig escapades took her a step closer. The petting zoo event had given Fox the chance to case out the situation. But Fox wasn't the mayor's only option; he'd have equally ambitious people to corrupt.

By the time the coffee was brewed, she'd finished formulating her plan. Although caffeine didn't agree with her anymore, the ritual died hard. That hot beverage made early mornings and tough challenges easier to face. Pouring the steaming liquid into travel mugs for Charlie and herself, she gathered her things in a shoulder bag, and headed out the door. Prima whined at her through the screen. The dog hated being left behind, and Hannah hated seeing her sad little face. How had she ever thought this dog homely? She was adorable. Leo was a sleek, mild-mannered sweetheart, but compared to Prima, he seemed almost two-dimensional. Her inquisitive expression, boundless energy and spunky persistence made her downright irresistible. Months earlier Hannah had put her name on Arianna's list for one of her gorgeous goldendoodle hybrids. It seemed like that spot in her life was now taken.

As if she knew her ratings were soaring, Prima trotted ahead to the barn, confident tail aloft. Once inside, Hannah forgot about the dog as she went about her chores. Normally, Prima just poked around in the barn, looking for rodents. When Hannah emerged from the chicken coop, however, the dog was nowhere to be seen. Charlie's truck crunched up the gravel driveway and she heaved a sigh of relief. With him on the property, it relieved pressure in every way. Now she was free to look for Prima. Then the dog could ride with her as she put up new posters for the missing pig.

On the porch, she heard the dog barking—short, high yaps of triumph. That was the bark Prima normally reserved for bragging over a dead mouse. Steeling herself for the sight of the dangling rodent, Hannah turned. Prima was far down the driveway, racing back and forth in short arcs. Ahead of her trotted Wilma at a brisk clip. Whenever the pig slowed, Prima applied encouragement by way of a well-placed nip.

"Wilma!" Hannah called. "You're home." And then, "Charlie!"

Charlie came out of the barn with his coffee in hand, and his face cracked into a grin when he saw the pair. "Don't move," he called to Hannah. "Looks like Prima's got this covered."

Sure enough, the terrier herded the pig through the wide barn doors, out the back door and right up to the gate of her own pen. Hannah tiptoed up behind as Charlie calmly unlatched the door and let the pig into the field.

Closing the door, he turned and grinned. "I love happy endings, don't you?"

Hannah knelt beside Prima and hugged her. "I sure do," she said. "And this one calls for a huge celebration."

THE OLD ORCHARD on the east side of the farm had been transformed into a fairyland. Charlie had rented a cherry picker, and the gang gathered to string thousands of lights in the squat, gnarled trees. The space between the two sections was perfect to set up 10 long tables, end to end.

"Build it and they will come," Duff said, setting candelabras on each table. "Although I'm still not sure why you're entertaining people who haven't really been supporting you."

"That's the general idea," Remi said, setting up folding chairs. "Memorial Day is one of our biggest events of the year."

"Dog Town can never resist a party," Flynn said, arranging flowers in crystal vases.

"Or free food," Sasha added, laying out real white china, rented from the local party supplier.

"Not to mention champagne," Ari said, setting flutes at each place setting. "Bubbles bring out the best in people."

"How did I get stuck on napkins?" Cori grumbled, rolling cutlery in linen squares.

"I assigned everyone according to their skills," Bridget said, smirking. As the manager of Bone Appetit Bistro, a popular little restaurant in town, she knew how to stage an event efficiently and Duff, Remi and Sasha added the flair.

"Agreed. My skills are better used elsewhere," Cori said, rising. "If you'll—"

"Sit," Bridget said. "And try taking off the gloves to improve your dexterity."

Flipping her the bird, Cori abandoned her post. "I'm going to make sure those animals are locked up tight. Why you'd bring a hundred people in here after what's happened is beyond me, Hannah."

"Community," Hannah said simply. She was setting party favors in the middle of each plate. There were tea candles and bone-shaped dog biscuits, all adorned with the Runaway Farm logo Flynn Strathmore had designed. "No one but our crew volunteered to search for Wilma. That told me I had work to do to build goodwill. Maybe the mayor can knock one person down easily enough, but it will be harder to unseat an army."

"You think one meal will do that?" Cori asked.

"Not just any meal," Bridget said. "She's spared no expense with this feast."

"There's just enough bubbly to get people dancing," Hannah said, gesturing to the dancefloor they'd pieced together beside the portable stage. "I had to pull in some favors to get this band on board. The lead singer's a dog lover, and I told him I'd donate to his favorite rescue."

"Dog dollars," Ari said. "The currency of our community."

"It's going to blow the town's Memorial Day parade out of the water," Sasha said, her eyes sparkling. "The tickets sold out in 10 minutes and crashed the website."

"I didn't want to charge anything, but it was the only way to limit the crowd," Hannah said. "With the proceeds going to charity, no one can complain."

"Someone can always complain," Bridget said. "My Thanksgiving Pageant is a huge hit, and there are always whiners. There's no pleasing everyone in Dog Town."

"Maybe not," Remi said. "Planning fresh fundraisers for the hospital is getting tougher all the time. But I still think most people in this town have big hearts. The mayor just gets them confused about their priorities."

"The opposite of what a good leader should do," Hannah said. "But let's see if we can't set a new tone."

The first wave of vehicles arrived. There were several trucks bearing more friends with willing hands. Mim and Carver, Tiller, Sullivan, Nick Springdale, and Sasha's boyfriend Griffin. Hannah, Bridget and Remi produced and directed what turned out to be an elegant event that was still lighthearted and fun. The men handled crowd control, making sure the guests observed protocol. Luckily it was a far different audience than the petting zoo had attracted. These people wore sundresses and sports jackets, and had children and dogs that behaved. At first, there was a hesitant formality, but Remi staged icebreakers, going from table to table with Hannah offering a fishbowl full of questions to spark conversation.

Finally, when everyone was digging into a barbeque feast that featured local foods from nearby Wolff County, Hannah joined her friends. They'd gathered near the twisted vine arch that served as the entryway to the event. Nick Springdale came over with a lawn chair and urged her to sit.

"I can't just yet," she said. "Probably not till it all ends well. I feel like everything rides on this, somehow."

"It doesn't," Nick said, smiling. "But if it did, you'd be gold. There's laughter, the clink of glasses, the clatter of cutlery and the sounds of dogs playing. What more could you want?"

Hannah held up her finger as children's voices rose in some playground song. "That's it," she said, smiling. "Now it's perfect. I came back for community, and to me, this is what it sounds like."

He offered her a sip of champagne and she shook her head. "Gotta stay sharp. No one likes a tipsy farmer."

"Best kind," he said. "As long as you're not driving a tractor."

"As if. Although Charlie's got the old one working again."

"If the event ends well, maybe we could take it on a moonlight ride later," Nick said. He leaned in close enough that Hannah could smell his aftershave. It seemed like a perfect blend of cedar and summer meadows. "I promised you driving lessons."

"Maybe I'll even take you up on that. In daytime, that is. And not on a tractor."

She leaned away from him. It was getting harder to resist him, but it had to be done. Nick would never be interested if he knew her secret and she couldn't lead him on. It wouldn't be fair to either of them. Besides, the last thing she needed was more drama, especially if it divided her friends in any way. At this point, her goal was clear: a solid foundation of unshakeable, harmonious relationships.

Nick held out his plate. "You need to eat something. It's going to be a long night."

She took a spare rib and nibbled on it. "Yum. That tastes right."

"Like community?" he asked, teasingly.

"Definitely. That's what I remember from childhood. Barbeque. Smokey ribs and sticky fingers from rib sauce. My mom hosted an open house every Memorial Day. Then she invited neighbors over most Sundays through the summer." She glanced up at him and grinned. "I hated the crowds then, of course. All those squealing kids that needed to be entertained. Somehow that job fell to me."

"I'm no fan of squealing children, either," he said. "Give me a nice pup, or even a grouchy pig, over kids any day."

The rib froze midway to Hannah's lips. So, Nick hated kids. Well, then he wasn't perfect, anyway, or at least not perfect for her. Her future featured at least one squealing kid—more if she could swing it—as well as nice pups and grouchy pigs.

He was staring at her, his hazel eyes dark in the fading light. "Everything okay?"

Nodding, she nibbled again on the rib. Now it tasted like disappointment. The delicious nostalgia that had filled her mouth and her heart moments earlier turned to gritty ash. She let the rib dangle from her saucy fingers, staring over Nick's shoulder at the crowd. So intent was she that she failed to notice a stealthy brown and white marauder sneaking up beside her. One tug and the rib was gone. Leo's white tail flashed in the twinkle lights as he vanished into the orchard.

"That felt like an organized hit," she told Nick.

"You're an easy mark," someone said. "Prima exploits you, too."

Cori had appeared behind them and Hannah wondered how much she had overheard. "Prima and I are working things out," she said. "The pig is a different circus."

"One thing at a time," Remi said, joining them. "Have you seen Leo?"

"He made off with a spare rib," Hannah told her. "I hope he can digest bones."

"He's eaten worse," Remi said, glancing around for him.

"You've got a hit on your hands tonight, Hannah," Duff said. "You must be pleased."

The crowd in the orchard applauded as the band took a break. "It's a relief," Hannah said. "If the reviews are good, maybe I'll think about expanding on this."

Remi's smile flashed in the dusk. "The inn we talked about?"

"Something like that," Hannah said. "It's definitely

more my speed than a petting farm. But it'll take a lot of work, and I'd need public buy-in to do it."

"You're on the way," Remi said, as Leo appeared at her side, his white face smeared in barbeque sauce. "You're ready to bust out, I can feel it."

She covered her mouth quickly, but Hannah just laughed. "You're right, my friend. You are so right."

CHAPTER FIFTEEN

A spectacular sunrise had given way to a gorgeous late May day. After completing her rounds of the henhouse, Hannah sat on the porch with Prima in her lap and a cup of tea in her hand, killing an hour before delivering eggs to the neighbors. In the three days since the Memorial Day event, the neighbors had started visiting her. On the counter inside sat three pies and half a dozen jars of preserves from the Wolff County side, and wine and store-bought cookies from neighbors on the Dorset Hills side. It was satisfying just to be on the radar of the Dog Town populace. The more she could build public sympathy, the better her chances of putting down roots and raising a happy family here. Resting her hand on her belly, still so flat it was hard to believe life grew inside, she said, "I'm doing what I can, Jellybean. Hang tight."

Prima nudged her hand, spilling the tea down the front of her white T-shirt. She tried to wring it out and ended up with a wrinkled mess. Then she leaned back in her chair and smiled. In her old life, she'd have jumped up to change.

Now it didn't feel like a rush at all. There was time to finish the remaining mouthfuls and let the sun warm her face.

The crunch of gravel made her turn. What now? More preserves, or a contractor come to make a pitch? News of her hopes to build a boutique inn had spread quickly, as any juicy bit of gossip did in Dorset Hills, even on the outskirts. One local builder had arrived before noon the day after the fete with a gift basket full of high-end treats and trinkets. The same builder had refused to return her call two weeks ago for smaller jobs, and he certainly wouldn't get her business now. She kept the gift basket, however, to support Remi's next fundraiser. It was a sign that the tide was turning and for that she was grateful.

Standing, she tried to push Prima into the house without accidentally releasing Duncan the parrot. After his brief taste of freedom, the bird now sat waiting for a chance to swoop out as the door opened. Prima refused to be shoved through a crack, and instead frolicked down the front stairs to greet the guest.

Hannah followed, and let out a long groan when she recognized the black sedan moving at a glacial pace.

"Good morning, Mayor," she said, as he rolled down the window and offered a bland smile. "What brings you to Runaway Farm today? A yen for fresh eggs?" She pointed to the basket on the lower step. "Your next omelet awaits."

He dismissed her suggestion with a wave. "Watching my cholesterol. I can't stay long anyway."

As if she'd meant to cook for him. "Well, that's a shame."

He turned the key in the ignition and sat in silence for a moment. "I'm not quite sure how to say this, Hannah. But there's been a complaint."

"A complaint?"

"Several, really. Calls to the Tattle Tail Hotline, mainly. I've heard you have an aggressive pig on the premises. And that said pig savaged a guest at your illegal free-for-all."

Hannah shoved her hands into the pocket of her jeans, then noticed the massive tea stain and crossed her arms instead. "Illegal what?"

"You need a permit for any public event in Dorset Hills. Even when there are no savage pigs in attendance."

She stared at him. "When I called City Hall, I was told I needed a permit for any event with more than 100 people on the site at one time. My events have been smaller than that. Much smaller, in the case of the petting zoo. There are family reunions bigger than that."

The mayor brushed at invisible dust on his lapels. "We reserve the right to make decisions on a case-by-case basis. Of course, any case with a savage pig would be turned down promptly."

"Sir. You've obviously received inaccurate information. The pig I rescued was actually baited by someone who got into the pen with her and played matador. Her hoof grazed the lady's shin when she tried to escape. I do have witnesses."

"None of them credible, I'm afraid." He smiled, revealing eyeteeth that looked strangely yellow in the morning sun. "The poor couple was terrified, and we can't take the chance of disease spreading around town—to people, or dogs."

Now Hannah put her hands on her hips, regardless of the tea stain. "You know perfectly well this pig is a threat to no one."

"I know this farm is a threat to public safety. And that's why you are no longer permitted to host events of any kind on the property. A pig bite spoiled the whole thing, I'm afraid. Animal Services wanted to apprehend her, but I declined. Since we're old friends, you and I, a warning would more than suffice."

The tea roiled in Hannah's stomach and she balled her fists. "Mayor Bradshaw, we really need to work this out. I want to invest in this property and this town, yet I feel blocked at every turn by silly plots and pranks. Isn't it time we sat down like professional business people? You used to run a successful business yourself, so I'm sure you realize what a nuisance these visits are."

He turned the key in the ignition. "If my visits are such a nuisance, I'll be on my way, Miss Pemberton." He put the car in reverse and let it roll backwards a yard or two before adding, "Just to be clear, if you have any notion of starting a business in hospitality, you'll need to go back to the drawing board. You will never get the permits you need."

She walked after the sedan and put a hand on the dusty hood, trying to stop him. He kept inching backwards, until she slapped the hood. "Mayor, you are being extremely shortsighted. I've done the research and this town desperately needs an upscale inn."

"That's where you're wrong," he said. "We've got plans... and they don't include an upscale resort on a hobby farm." He leaned out the window and eyed the stains on her T-shirt. "I guess 'upscale' is all in the eye of the beholder."

He pressed the accelerator and the car slipped away from her hand. She swung her leg back to take a kick and thought better of it. Why give him the satisfaction of falling onto her dusty driveway?

Dangling his fingers out of the driver's window, he offered a low wave.

That was his biggest mistake. Prima took a lunge at his

hand and when she landed, there was a glint of gold in her teeth.

The mayor slammed his foot on the brakes, came forward again and almost hit Hannah. Leaning out the window, he yelled, "Give me back my ring, you varmint!"

Prima spun twice in a frenzy of excitement, and Hannah reached for her. "Stay. Drop it."

But the dog whirled off like a canine dervish, taking the ring with her.

"I'll get it back for you," Hannah said. "I'll drop it off at City Hall."

He glared at her and then put the car in reverse. "Have it professionally cleaned, please, and send it by courier."

He'd barely left the property before Prima romped back into view... without the ring. Sighing, Hannah walked all over the driveway and into the bushes where the dog had slipped away. It was no use. She would never find the mayor's ring in all that dust. The only option was renting a metal detector. Add another task to her long list of farm chores.

Wrestling Prima into the house, she finally left to deliver the eggs—a chore that had become a pleasure.

The noon sun blinded her as she raced down the driveway in her golf cart. She should have taken a moment to grab her sunglasses or a hat, but she needed to escape for a few hours. By the time she got back, the emotional dust from the mayor's visit would have settled.

Careening down the driveway, she started to feel a little better, a little lighter. Then she turned the last bend and screamed. She slammed her foot on the brake, but it was too late. If she stayed on the driveway, she'd smash into the large brown animal standing in the middle of it.

So she sent the golf cart into the ditch.

REMI PUSHED the curtains aside and came back into the hospital cubicle.

"They said you can go now." She handed Hannah a basket containing her sneakers, jeans and stained T-shirt. "You are so lucky, Hannah."

"Lucky? I have a camel wandering around loose on my property. How is that lucky?"

Remi took out the T-shirt, eyed it, and shook her head. "First, it's not a camel, but an alpaca. And second, it's not loose but in one of your new paddocks."

Hannah swung her legs over the bed and untied the hospital gown. "I fail to see how an alpaca is any luckier than a camel. And having exotic livestock dumped on my property is definitely not lucky. Especially now that the mayor's thrown down the gauntlet. Can you believe someone tied it to a stake in the gravel?"

"Forget the alpaca for a second. What's lucky is that you drove your golf cart into a ditch and survived. You're all right. The baby is all right."

Holding a finger to her lips, Hannah said, "The curtains have ears."

"And you can't afford to be taking risks like that when you're expecting. At least everything looks fine."

Tears started up in Hannah's eyes but she blinked them back. It was a relief that all was well. Maybe Flynn Strathmore's drawing was right, and it was the daughter she'd always wanted. But there was a long road ahead before that child made an appearance, and by then she needed to have her ducks in a row. They were decidedly not in a row right now.

"Would it have been better to hit the alpaca, do you

think?" she said, pulling the stained T-shirt over her head. "Frankly, I think the ditch was the right choice. Even though I broke most of the eggs. What a mess."

Remi sighed. "There was no good choice. I'm so angry someone dumped an alpaca on your property. Bob got his fair share of abandoned cats, dogs and chickens, but there was nothing on this scale in recent years."

Hopping on one foot, Hannah pulled on her jeans. "Do you think it's a setup?"

"Of course it's a setup." Remi tossed balled-up socks at her one by one. "The only question is, who's behind it?"

"The mayor, of course. Although he'd just left when it happened."

Pushing Hannah down on the stretcher, Remi perched beside her. "We know he wants to scuttle Runaway Farm, but adding to the menagerie seems like a risky move. It's not like he doesn't have other devious devices."

Lacing her sneakers, Hannah grunted. "Who then?"

"We'll need the Mafia to help with that. They're all waiting for us, so let's get going."

In the hallway, they bumped into Mim Gardiner, who was in her nursing scrubs. She wrapped Hannah in a hug. "I'm so glad everything's fine."

The sheen of tears in Mim's eyes told Hannah the secret circle had expanded. "You know."

"About the new camel, yes," Mim said, grinning as she spoke in a secret code. "It couldn't happen to a nicer farmer."

"It's an alpaca, apparently." Hannah reluctantly let Mim settle her in a wheelchair for the ride out. "That makes all the difference."

"I'm sure you'll make a fine owner to this new addition," Mim said, pushing the wheelchair into a private alcove.

"Maybe it's a girl. I love my boy, but I always wanted a girl, too."

Hannah nodded, tears welling again. "I won't lie. A girl alpaca is exactly what I wanted. I just hope I can handle it."

Mim put an arm around her shoulders. "Of course you can. I can tell you from experience that you never think you're up to raising an alpaca, but somehow it all works out. I even managed to raise a human son on my own without completely ruining him. And I can also tell you that the timing is never perfect for things like this."

"The timing was probably just right," Hannah said. "I wanted a... an alpaca very much and had reason to think I should do it sooner rather than later." She looked around to make sure no one was eavesdropping. "Health reasons. But that doesn't mean I don't have doubts. Especially in the current environment."

"It's going to be fine," Mim told her. "Alpacas are surprisingly versatile. They thrive wherever there's love. You have the financial means, too, which takes away one big worry. I'd say you're well ahead in the alpaca game."

Hannah nodded. "I can handle an alpaca as well as the next woman, I guess. And there's no way in hell I'm letting Bill Bradshaw put my alpaca in jeopardy."

"That's the spirit," Mim said, wheeling Hannah out of the alcove and down the hall. "But you've got to be careful, too. No more driving into ditches."

"I've heard it takes a village to raise an alpaca," Remi added, as they approached the revolving front door. "You've got that, Hannah. We may not have special expertise in alpaca management—yet—but we won't let you down. I promise."

Hannah got up and they wrapped each other into a

triple hug, holding on so long that someone deliberately nudged them aside to push through the door.

"Get a room," the woman said.

They turned and saw Fox Spinner, with her arm in a sling.

"Hard day in the office?" Hannah asked.

"Something like that," Fox said. "You know, sometimes I actually miss the farm. I could breathe there."

"But you've got the mayor, now," Hannah said. "His friendship must make up for the clean country air."

Fox eyed Hannah's stained shirt and dirty jeans and smirked before turning. "No more princess, Princess."

Hannah thought about getting the last word, but the revolving door cut her off.

CHAPTER SIXTEEN

After dinner that evening, a convoy of vehicles pulled up in front of the barn and parked. Bridget, Cori and the rest of the Mafia spilled out of the lime-green van, along with Ari and Sasha who were still viewed as honorary members, at least by Cori. This irked them both no end, as they gave their all to any rescue escapade. Hannah, on the other hand, was happy with a peripheral role, alongside Flynn, Mim and Remi. She had funded many Mafia exploits without asking questions, figuring the less she knew, the less she could trip up under scrutiny. And the Mafia was always under scrutiny. Kinney Butterfield, their friend in the Canine Corrections Department, had let them know that there was a fat digital file filled with information about them. Having decided to build an inn here at Runaway Farm, Hannah couldn't afford to have a prominent place in that fat file. She'd need permits, and builders, and most of all publicity. The hospitality industry was tough enough without government moving against her. And while she could afford to raise a family without an active business, she very much wanted her child to see a happy, engaged mother contributing to society. Spending a short time in idle wealth after her mother's passing had shown her that floating without a mission was a recipe for depression. Only volunteer work had brought her out of a serious tailspin.

Now, she was most definitely engaged and committed, and by the time her baby made her debut late in the year, she intended to have wheels in motion. Her child would grow up in a quaint, classy inn bringing the farm experience to city folk.

A grey Prius pulled up behind Bridget's van and Kinney Butterfield got out. Kinney generally tried to walk the line between the foolish policies of her civic employer and the common sense that had made her a rescuer long before she went over to what Cori described as the "dark side."

The last vehicle to arrive was Nick's red truck. It was still rolling slowly when the passenger door opened and a woman with curly red hair jumped down. Arms outstretched, she ran around the truck and was instantly enveloped by the crowd, and screams of "Evie!" and "You're back!"

Evelyn Springdale, Nick's sister, had only been gone since Easter—and she'd only been a Dog Town resident for a scant month before that. Nonetheless, she was much-loved and had been missed. Hannah hoped they'd feel the same way about her one day, but there was no question that Evie had paid her dues. While working in public relations for the City, she'd managed to unravel a twisty rescue challenge that put Dog Town in a poor light, and save face for the mayor while doing it. The gambit had almost killed her, but now she looked radiant.

Coming up to Hannah, Evie grabbed both her hands. "I came as soon as I could."

"Are you all right?" Hannah asked. "It can take months to get over a concussion."

Evie's freckled face was still pale, but her beautiful green eyes danced. "I just have to pace myself. The doctor cleared me for normal life."

"But life in Dog Town is never normal," Hannah said. "The fact that you've just arrived for a Mafia strategy session proves that."

"It feels good to be home," Evie said, grinning. "Plotting and scheming and helping good people and pets. That'll help me bounce back like nothing else. I just hope banging up my head didn't affect my tactical skills."

"You've got us for that," Cori said. "There's a lot of cognitive capital on this porch."

Hannah looked around at everyone pulling up lawn chairs and smiled. "There most certainly is."

"Cognitive capital?" Evie said. "I like that."

Nick looked a little out of his element surrounded by women. Sullivan, Tiller, Carver and Griffin tried to avoid the worst of Mafia business, since their jobs relied on good relationships throughout Dorset Hills. It was always a fine balance between doing the right thing and supporting their partners, and keeping their noses clean enough to get contracts. Somehow they managed. Nick had to be even more careful, with his government IT contract, but she supposed he wanted to stay close to Evie while she was still recovering.

"Show me around," Evie said, gesturing to the barn. "I want to meet the key players."

Cori started to get up, and Evie shook her head. "Sit. I

want to hear it from Hannah. Too many voices make my head ache."

Cori raised her gloved hand and Remi forced it down. "Never mind."

"She's a peach," Evie said, following Hannah along the stone path to the entrance of the barn. "But I've missed her. In fact, I missed everyone while my mother was hovering over me with ice packs and hot tea."

"Especially Jon, I assume," Hannah said, waggling her eyebrows suggestively.

Jon was the veterinarian who helped Evie through her big escapade, and they seemed like a great match.

"Definitely. And Roberto, too," Evie said, grinning. "That cat and I have bonded in ways I wouldn't have thought possible. Nick says he kept running home from his place to wait for me at mine. Every night he'd go over and bring him back. For a month."

"That's pretty sweet," Hannah said. "Of both of them."

They were in the barn now, and Evie looked around. "He's a good guy, you know. My brother."

Hannah glanced at her quickly. "I do know. He's been wonderful through all of this."

"But...?" Evie said. "You're not interested in him that way?"

Sighing, Hannah led her first to Florence, the mare. "I'm not in a position to date right now. That's all. There's a lot on my plate, as you can tell."

Evie cocked her head, staring at Hannah as if she could hear all that she wasn't saying. Then she nodded. "I understand."

"I don't think someone like Nick will stay single for long," Hannah said. "In fact, he was with a pretty girl at the spring fair."

"Daughter of a client," Evie said. "And he's not interested."

"Oh, well. It's not my business, I guess."

"It could be your business," Evie said, grinning. "A sister worries, you know."

"I do know," Hannah said. "I worry about James, too. I just want him to come home and meet a nice girl. Somehow everything gets so complicated in Dorset Hills."

"It does." Evie stroked the mare's nose. "But I've seen serious knots unfurl given time and some fancy political footwork." She looked down at her strappy sandals. "Speaking of footwork, I should have worn flats."

"Steel-toed work boots," Hannah said. "It's the first thing I learned after taking some awkward spills."

"I don't really do boots," Evie said. "Easier to evade notice in heels, I've found."

Hannah laughed, relieved the tense moment had passed. "Nothing I do escapes notice, apparently."

Evie walked ahead of her on the balls of her feet. She stopped to lean over a pen to pat a lamb. "That's exactly what we have to use, Hannah."

"The lamb?" Hannah said, confused.

"The lamb, yes," Evie said, heading outside. "The kibitzing goats, the mellow cows, the sweet mare. Even the grumpy pig." She spun around in the wide area behind the barn, arms wide like Maria on the mountaintop in The Sound of Music. "All of it. When nothing you do escapes notice, you grab that spotlight and use it."

"How so? All it's got me so far is warnings, a pignapping, and an abandoned alpaca. I'm afraid of what your spotlight might bring."

Evie pulled her phone out of her pocket and hit the

video button. "All of this is so picturesque. People will love it."

"People? What people?"

Continuing to film, Evie said. "Your fans. They'll love this stuff."

"I have no fans, last time I checked. I don't even have a social media account."

"We'll change that today," Evie said, beckoning. "Introduce me to wonderful Wilma. And tell me how you two met."

"Turn that thing off," Hannah said, walking ahead of her.

"Okay. So, you were fresh from New York City. Bought the farm, so to speak."

"Very funny." Hannah picked her way through the muddy yard, expecting to lose Evie in her heels. There hadn't been much rain lately but the potholes never dried up. "But it did feel like a bit of a death wish, sometimes."

"So you were at the Dorset Hills spring fair when you locked eyes with this pig…"

"The poor thing," Hannah said, crossing her arms on the top rung of the paddock and staring in at Wilma. "She was neglected. Filthy."

"Aren't pigs supposed to be filthy?"

"Her skin was a mess. I don't think she'd seen sunlight in a year. And she was malnourished. I couldn't leave her there. So I bought her and brought her here."

"And then she knocked you into the mud," Evie said.

"She did. Ingrate." Hannah laughed. "I still love her. When she was set loose I was beside myself. She's expecting, you know."

"Piglets. Adorable."

"We've built her a birthing suite. These babies are going to live in pig luxury."

Evie laughed, too. "But will you be able to part with any of them?"

"That's the problem. You get attached."

"Did you ever anticipate getting attached to pigs?" Evie asked. "When you were living in that NYC apartment?"

"No, I most certainly did not." Hannah turned to find Evie's phone trained on her. "Evie, stop. Why on earth are you filming me?"

Evie pressed the off button and lowered her phone. "For your social media channel. Just something casual and fun. I'm thinking of calling it 'The Princess and the Pig.'"

Hannah laughed, and then choked on it when Evie raised her eyebrows to convey she wasn't joking.

"No way," Hannah said. "Uh-uh. I am not shooting a reality show called The Princess and the Pig."

Hanging over the pig pen, Evie filmed Wilma, who was staring at them with tiny eyes. "It's a guaranteed crowd-pleaser. The likeable heiress and the grumpy pig. I predict a hit."

"You predict wrong. I value my privacy too much for that, Evie. What would be the point, anyway?"

Placing one high heel on the lowest rung of the fence, Evie hoisted herself up and sat on the top rail. "You know what I do, right?"

"Public relations?"

"Exactly. I worked for the mayor. I know what motivates him. I know what terrifies him. And The Princess and the Pig will do the latter."

Hannah winced at the title. "How will that do anything more than make him laugh at me?"

"People will laugh *with* you, not at you. You're a very sympathetic character, and so are all the animals here at Runaway Farm. If you were on social media regularly, you'd know that people eat this kind of thing up. They'll be fascinated with a behind-the-scenes look at a hobby farm, and the elegant heiress who gave up a sweet life in the city to save animals in need. And the more people who follow you, the more public support you'll have. It will weaken the mayor's position."

Hannah crossed her arms and stared at Evie. "There's got to be another way to weaken his position besides putting me under public scrutiny."

"There's always another way," Evie said. "But this is the best. And the fastest."

Leaning into the pen, Hannah scratched Wilma's broad back gently with a forked stick. The pig leaned into it, snorting gently. When Hannah looked up, Evie was filming again.

Hannah grabbed the phone and turned off the camera. "I've been looking into other ways. I have someone checking out the mayor, for example."

"A private investigator? What did you find?"

"Not enough," Hannah admitted. "I know where Princess is—the poodle he dumped. And there are some negative reports about the poor dogs he's kicked out of town for misbehaving. Plus plenty of dirt on his cronies."

Evie nodded. "All potentially useful. But using that information would be taking the low road when we could take the high road instead. What road do you prefer?"

"I don't drive, as you probably know."

"I do. It's a theme of the show, actually."

"Quit talking about the show as if it's a given."

Swinging her feet, Evie looked at her muddy toes. "I'm

not afraid to get dirty if I have to. Politics is like wrestling a greased pig."

Leaning against the fence, Hannah sighed. "My mother didn't raise me to play political games."

"She created art to put a smile in people's heart, and she wanted you to do the same."

"A reality show isn't art. And other than art exhibitions, my mom was a private person."

Hopping down from the fence, Evie snatched her phone from Hannah. "Let me ask you this: would your mom have encouraged you to do your best for Runaway Farm? Would she have backed you in getting really creative about winning right now?"

Shoving off the fence, Hannah stared at Wilma. "Would she have backed The Princess and the Pig? The answer is a definite no." She started walking back to the barn. "She would have challenged me to aim higher."

"Well," Evie said, following her, phone raised again. "I didn't know her, but like most moms, she'd probably want you to do what felt right."

Turning, Hannah covered the phone. "Exactly. And The Princess and the Pig feels all wrong."

CHAPTER SEVENTEEN

"Think out loud, Hannah. Turn this way. And for pity's sake, smile."

Hannah forced her lips into a strained arc. "I'm collecting eggs. And what I think is that I hate every moment of this. And probably that Evie Springdale and I can't be friends anymore."

Evie lowered her professional-caliber video camera. "Sourpuss. You'll scare the hens off laying. And since I already know it's your favorite part of farm ownership, why not sell it?"

"I'm not selling anything." Hannah squeezed the egg in her hand so hard it cracked. She shook yolk off her fingers and cursed mildly.

"No cursing." Evie raised her camera again. "That'll create editing work for me later. But the broken egg is good stuff. Keep that up, princess."

"Do not call me princess."

"The day you come out to collect eggs without a full face of makeup is the day I stop calling you princess," Evie said. "You think the hens care about your eyeliner?"

Hannah glared at her. "I can't believe I ever thought I liked you."

Evie zoomed in for a close up. "You like me now but you'll *love* me later, when Mayor Bradshaw comes begging you to take your show offline. Won't that moment be sweet?"

"If it ever happens. In the meantime, I'll be mortified. I keep thinking about what James would say."

"If your brother is like my brother, he'd say do what you have to do, and give it your all."

Hannah rolled her eyes. "That doesn't sound like the Nick I know."

Lowering the camera, Evie grinned. "Wouldn't you like to get to know Nick better? Every show needs a love interest to keep the ladies coming back."

"Cute farm animals aren't enough?" Hannah wiped her hand on her jeans. "I'm thinking the alpaca will be the big draw."

"Can't wait to meet her. But nothing sells like a hot guy. Or better yet, a few hot guys vying for your attention."

"The Princess and the Rural Hotties?"

Circling her with camera raised, Evie said, "Finally, you're getting it. And thank goodness, because I can't do this all day without getting a monster of a migraine."

The frustration drained out of Hannah instantly. "Are you okay? Why don't we take a break?"

"I'll be fine. Especially if you could just suck it up and act like this is serious. Or seriously funny, at least. Lighten up. Educate people in an entertaining way."

"I don't know enough about farming to educate people."

"You just need to know more than they do. The people who are watching probably know zilch about hobby farms."

Swallowing what she really wanted to say, Hannah took

a deep breath and then made a sweeping motion with one hand. Pointing to the floor, she said, "Meet Aladdin, folks. He's a hero here in the henhouse. The guy all the girls want. The rooster of every pullet's dreams."

Evie gave her the thumbs up, and then made a rolling motion with her hand to keep going.

"Without Aladdin," Hannah continued, "these girls wouldn't be inspired to lay an egg a day. All he needs to do is strut around the coop and the eggs just keep coming." She stared directly at the lens. "I'm not sure exactly how those eggs arrive, but I suspect Aladdin's got it pretty easy by comparison."

Evie's camera shook with her laughter.

Turning, Hannah introduced various hens, starting with her favorite, Jemima, the fluffy white silky bantam. Then she located as many eggs as she could to correspond to their owners.

"I learned about all of this just as you might expect... by googling. I researched hens and eggs and backyard chicken coops. I even went to a baby name site and came up with 43 names so that each hen would feel special. Corny or what?"

Evie's free hand kept signalling to go on.

"How lucky am I?" Hannah asked the camera. "Each and every day I get an Easter egg hunt in my own backyard. Then, most days, I deliver the spoils to my neighbors. We'll do that a little later."

The camera bobbed up and down in agreement.

"But first, why don't we go out and meet the rest of the Runaway Farm family?" She walked out of the henhouse backwards, still facing the camera, and led Evie into the barn, stopping beside the horse's stall. "You already know Florence the mare. She's our grand dame, and she retired here after a very unpleasant time in her life about 10 years ago. She's blind, and her only job now is to accept treats and carry the occasional child around a ring." Florence nickered and nuzzled Hannah's hair, creating a nest of tangles on one side. Trying to smooth it down, she escorted Evie's camera from pen to outdoor paddock with a tidbit about each inhabitant. "Just two to go," she said, heading to a small paddock isolated from the rest. "When we get a new arrival, they need to be on their own for a bit to make sure they're healthy before being integrated into the farm ecosystem. That's why Alvina the alpaca's here on her own. It won't be for a second longer than necessary, though, because alpacas are herd animals and may actually die of loneliness if left alone too long." She glanced at the camera. "Isn't that sad? And we think there's a good chance Alvina was isolated and perhaps even abused, because she was very jumpy when she got here a few days ago." Gesturing to the animal, she said, "And when I say 'arrived,' I mean dumped. Abandoned. Discarded. It breaks my heart that for the past 10 years, people have been casting off animals at Runaway Farm like old garbage. Bob Hess, the previous owner, rehabilitated and rehomed over a hundred of them. In my eyes, he was a hero. And it's an honor to carry on the tradition." The alpaca came to the fence, hoping for treats, and Hannah draped her arm around its neck.

"If you're like me," she said, "you might wonder about the difference between an alpaca and a llama, both of whom belong to the camelid family. Alpacas are smaller and—to my mind anyway—cuter. They have rounder ears and bigger eyes, and a nice range of coat colors. Their wool is prized." The alpaca nuzzled the other side of her head, so that her hair was uniformly puffy and snarled. "What I found most interesting is that llamas make better livestock guardians. You can put a llama out to graze with sheep and they'll fend off predators like coyotes. Isn't that interesting? Alpacas aren't nearly as useful for that." She turned to look at Alvina. "Sorry, girl. You're no guard dog."

The animal's soft brown eyes met hers for a moment and then Alvina reared back. There was an awkward pause, a funny gurgling sound, and then warm fluid hit Hannah full in the face.

"What the—?"

She wiped her face on her sleeve and saw greenish goop on the chambray fabric. Blinking into the camera, she said, "Living in New York, it's not unusual to be spit on now and then. It happened to me twice. But never full in the face, and never with such volume. Just so you know, members of the camelid family sometimes regurgitate the contents of their stomach when they're angry or scared. If you're wondering whether it stinks, the answer is hell yeah." She gave a sniff. "It smells like yesterday's grass, festering and fermented. Luckily it didn't burn my eyes, but I think it's worth noting that safety goggles are probably an excellent idea around camera-shy alpacas. Stick around, folks. It's just one thrill after another here. We'll be right back with The Princess and the Pig."

Slicing her index finger across her throat, Hannah turned and threw up.

"GOOD GRACIOUS, you're a natural. A star in the making," Evie said. "I had no idea."

Hannah stared at the hay on the ground, her head still between her knees. Charlie knelt beside her and offered a damp rag and a chipped mug full of water. His hands were bruised and there was a white bandage on his right arm. Alpaca management wasn't a cakewalk for him, either.

"Do you miss the insurance business, Charlie?" she asked.

"Never," he said, laughing. "There's never a dull moment around here."

Evie knelt as Charlie got up.

"Please tell me you cut before I barfed," Hannah said.

"Consider it cut," Evie said. "We don't want to alienate our viewers with vomit."

"What's that about vomit?"

The deep voice belonged to Nick Springdale, and Hannah kept her head down, wiping a sad tale from her face with the rag. Between the alpaca spit, the matted hair and the nausea, it was hard to believe she'd ever looked worse.

"Are you okay?" he asked.

"Fine," she muttered, picking at the ground. "Never better. Just looking for a needle in a haystack."

"You already found him," Nick said. "I'm that rare perfect man who's as much at home on a farm as in a boardroom."

Evie snorted. "Since when? Last time I checked, you were a one-dog man. You don't even like my cat."

"How's your head, Evs?" he asked. "You haven't been the same since your concussion. I guess you've forgotten that I'm everyman—able to morph into what a good woman needs."

"Now *I'm* going to barf," Evie said. "Who stole my brother while I was gone?"

"Keep your cynicism to yourself," he said.

Hannah saw his boots beside her and then he knelt

down. "Let me give you a hand," he said. "Do you want to go inside?"

She shook her head. "I'm just taking a moment to recover from the grossest experience of my entire life."

"It was amazing," Evie said. "I couldn't have asked for better footage. This is going to send our premiere for The Pig and the Princess off the charts."

"Hey! I should get top billing," Hannah grumbled. "That pig is nothing without me."

Nick laughed. "I think she's getting her spark back."

Taking a deep breath, Hannah looked up, and said, "The show must go on."

Evie zoomed in for a close up. "Atta girl. Let's go meet your competition now, okay?"

Nick helped Hannah to her feet, and guided her out to the pig pen, like a knight in denim armor.

Running her hands through her tangled hair as best she could, Hannah switched on her smile. "You've probably wondered why we named the show The Princess and the Pig. Well, it all started with Wilma. She was my first official rescue after taking over Runaway Farm. I confess I arrived here with a bit of a princess attitude. I was a fan of yoga. Art. Keeping up appearances. I didn't see myself actually getting my hands dirty on day-to-day farm work. I intended to keep the status quo here, and no more." She gestured to the pig, and Evie zoomed in. "Enter Wilma. I saw her at a fair, and this was one sad, skinny pig. I knew I had the means to do something for her. So I bought her and brought her home."

Nick tried to stop her, but she climbed the fence and hopped into the pen. Wilma gave a few snuffling snorts that sounded like a warning. Hannah moved even further from the pig. It would be easy enough to jump out of harm's reach.

"I didn't know she was pregnant. I didn't know she was grumpy. I just knew she was in poor shape. A few weeks later, she's seen the vet and is on the mend. Is she still grumpy? You bet. I can't blame her, considering what she's been through."

Wilma stared up at the camera and pawed the mud. Charlie came out of the barn with a couple of apples and threw them into the pen, and the pig sniffed one, considering.

"Wilma and I, and all the other animals, live on the outskirts of Dorset Hills," Hannah continued. "It's known as the best place on earth for dogs and dog lovers, and it's my hometown. I came back for the wonderful sense of community that permeates this town. We have a civic leader who puts animal welfare at the top of the agenda. That's something I knew I could stand behind."

Wilma shoved the apple aside and started a slow trot in Hannah's direction. She didn't wait around this time. Instead she started to run back to the fence. Her boot hit one of the apples, squished it and slid. Arms spinning, she went down on one knee and then collapsed onto her side.

"Animal welfare," she said, barely missing a beat. "It's something I can stand behind, or even lie under if need be."

Nick leapt over the fence in one bound and helped her up, while Wilma made a broad circle, still snorting.

"One day, this grumpy pig might turn into a princess," Hannah said, staring into Evie's camera. "Let's hope it doesn't go the other way."

CHAPTER EIGHTEEN

E vie's wild red hair blew around her face as she drove the golf cart behind them, holding the camera high.

"This is a bad idea," Hannah said, from the passenger seat of Nick's truck.

"Relax, it'll be fun," he said, turning to give her a playful smile.

"Said no one ever who's over 30 and learning to drive."

"You already know how to drive. You've been driving around in a golf cart for two weeks."

"During which time I dented Sally's cart and your truck, not to mention the shameful loss of three dozen eggs.

"Nothing great happens without breaking a few eggs," he said. "Someone famous said that, right?"."

"Well, this beast isn't a golf cart." She tapped the dashboard. "And there's a lot more to break in here than eggs. Like both our heads, for example."

"Evie picked the perfect place," he said. "There's nothing but corn and rye to run down. Besides, you underestimate yourself."

She shook her head. "Who drives stick anymore

anyway? Did you have to pay extra to forgo automatic transmission?"

"I did have to wait six weeks for a special order. But people who really love driving still want a manual transmission."

Looking over her shoulder, she watched Evie raise the camera over her head in a salute. "Anything for ratings, I guess."

"The show's going great," he said. "Three episodes and already 20,000 followers. You really are a natural."

"People love pratfalls," she said. "And alpaca spit, as it turns out."

"They love animals, and they love someone who's willing to make sacrifices to help them. Getting semi-digested greens in your eyes is quite a sacrifice, in my books."

Hannah nodded. "I've never looked worse. Your sister has a talent for riches to rags stories."

"You look great," he said, slowing. "Anyway, this must be it."

"One empty field looks the same as another to me."

"It's opposite Sally Taylor's driveway. That's what she said."

Hannah brightened as they turned left into the field. It was freshly tilled and spacious. There was literally nothing she could hit for a half a mile on all sides. Surely she could navigate around an empty field without mishap. Why people would log on to watch that happen was beyond her, but so far the show was doing exactly what they intended: attracting attention and fans for Runaway Farm. Evie clearly knew what she was doing, and for that reason, Hannah was willing to go along with her schemes without asking too many questions.

In the middle of the field, Nick put the truck in park and jumped out. He ran around and managed to open the passenger door before Hannah could, then helped her jump down. Evie filmed all of it, of course. She was playing up every romantic angle she could find, including the hot handyman who'd repaired a fence earlier. It seemed like the camera had lingered on his butt far too long, but Hannah had decided to save her arguments for bigger things.

"Up you go," Nick said, helping Hannah climb behind the wheel and then jumping up on the running board to adjust the seat. Evie's camera poked into the open passenger door to capture everything. Nick was so close to Hannah that she held her breath. She found his summer meadow scent seductive, but distracting. Luckily he'd be seated properly before the truck was in gear.

If she could ever get the truck in gear.

A few minutes later, Nick said, "Deep breaths, Hannah. The truck's in neutral. Put your left foot on the clutch and press down. Now, move the gearshift to first. Ease off the clutch at the same time as you press down on the accelerator with your right foot."

"It's so complicated."

"Don't worry. You'll soon get a feel for it."

"*I* never did," Evie said, from the truck's tiny backseat. "When Dad tried to teach me, I got carsick from all the lurching."

"Fantastic," Hannah said. "All I need is more reasons to throw up."

"It'll be fine," Nick said. "Evie, just keep quiet and do your thing. Don't distract Hannah from the task at hand."

"Or at foot," Hannah said. "Now I see why you made me put on these cowboy boots this morning, Evie. I can barely feel the pedal. I'm sure that'll make for more drama."

"Rolling," Evie said.

Pressing down on the gas, Hannah eased up on the clutch, and the engine screamed. Nick literally flinched beside her. The truck lurched forward a few inches and then stalled.

"It's okay, it's okay," he said. "Try again."

Hannah tried again.

And again.

After the fifth stall, she gave a strangled cry of frustration. "I can't do this."

"Sure you can." Nick's voice was as calm and smooth as the warm May afternoon. "First time you moved an inch. Last time you moved a full yard. You're getting it, Hannah."

His confidence renewed her courage. She went through the steps one more time and finally—finally!—the truck started rolling.

Quickly.

It rolled very quickly indeed.

"What do I do now?" Her voice spiked as the truck hurtled toward the opening in the field.

"Steer! Turn right, turn right, turn right."

He was gesturing wildly with his left hand. So she turned left.

"No, right," he said, still gesticulating with his left hand.

She pulled around in a full circle.

"Wow, a donut!" Evie said, her tone a blend of terror and excitement.

Hannah straightened out, still pressing the gas to keep from stalling. The truck shot through the opening in the fence and across the highway.

There was just enough time for the twin screams of brother and sister before the truck ran right into Sally Taylor's mailbox, knocking the post right over. The truck stalled as Hannah pressed the brake and came to a shuddering stop.

"Cut!" Evie called, to no one in particular, since she was the only crew.

Turning to Nick, Hannah said, "I'm so sorry."

"It's okay." His normally warm voice had cooled by several degrees. "That's what fenders are for."

"For running down mailboxes?" Hannah gave a shaky laugh.

"You're breaking mine in well," he said, laughing too.

They both jumped out of the truck and Evie followed, camera rolling again. She zoomed in on the front of the truck and looked almost disappointed that there was nothing more than a second small dent.

"We'd best go tell Sally," she said. "I'll get the golf cart."

Nick pulled the truck around and proceeded down the drive ahead of his sister, with Hannah riding shotgun in the golf cart. The jaunty yellow mailbox, still on its pole, stuck out of the bed of the pickup. The little red flag was up.

Sally came out her front door, and her mouth dropped. "What happened here?"

"A mailbox mishap," Hannah said. "I'll replace it, of course. I'm so sorry, Sally."

The older woman just laughed. "It's no problem. Just leave it by the steps. I'll put it in the shed and get Charlie to give me a hand setting it back up." She took a close look at Hannah. "Honey, you don't look well. Come inside for a glass of water."

"I—I think I will, if you don't mind," Hannah said.

As she trailed after Sally up the stairs, she glanced back and saw Nick carrying the mailbox to the shed, while Evie followed with the camera rolling.

Inside, Sally pushed Hannah into a seat at the kitchen table. "You look like you've seen a ghost. What's up?"

"My life did flash before my eyes," Hannah said. "The standard transmission defeated me, I'm afraid."

"Let me guess: it's something your friend cooked up for the new show."

Taking a sip of the water, Hannah nodded. "Anything to raise the profile of Runaway Farm."

"It certainly seems to be working." Sally pulled her hair back and winced. Her forefinger was wrapped in a white bandage.

"What happened there?" Hannah asked.

"Cut it slicing an apple," Sally said. "Took a couple of stitches, but on the mend already."

There was a knock at the front door and then Evie slipped inside. "Do you mind?" she asked, nodding at the camera.

"What are neighbors for?" Sally asked, smiling.

Hannah took a deep breath, and repeated her apology about the mailbox on camera. "I promise I'll make it up to you, Sally," she said. "You'll never want for eggs for your entire life."

"I love scrambled," Sally said. "You can't get anywhere in life without breaking a few eggs, it seems."

NICK PRESSED the pedal down hard on the way back to the farm. At first, Hannah thought he was angrier at her than he had let on. But when she saw his eyes darting repeatedly up at the rear- view mirror, she realized he was trying to shake his sister, who was once again following on the golf cart.

"I really am sorry," she said. "If there's any damage to your transmission, I'll have the work done."

"I'm sure it's fine," he said. "They build trucks like this to take a beating."

She braced herself on the dash. "Are you trying to prove it's a rocket as well? We're about to achieve liftoff."

Glancing over his shoulder, he said, "I just wanted to lose Evie so we could have a moment to talk."

"Oh? About what?" Excitement collided with dread in her belly and made her queasy again. Baby didn't like her flirting, perhaps.

"I just feel like Evie railroaded you into this online show. She's really pushy sometimes. Ten years as a political fixer can do that to you."

"I trust her instincts." Hannah rolled down her window and let the wind blow back her hair. "But that doesn't mean I like my starring role in The Princess and the Pig." She turned and grinned at him. "All my co-star needs to do is stand there and grunt."

Nick slowed before turning into her driveway. The potholes had multiplied and deepened with all the trucks coming and going, and he let the truck coast over them gently.

"You can pull out at any time, remember." He glanced at her. "What does the little one think about all this? Is she on board?"

"The little one?" Her stomach did a triple flip. *How did he know?*

"You know... the one with the gloves. She seems to call most of the shots with Evie's friends. Bit of a temper, and trigger-happy flipping fingers."

"Oh, Cori!" Hannah's laugh rang out and he smiled, too. "She's not a fan of the idea. Evie had to threaten her somehow to keep her off 'set' when we're shooting. The Mafia needs to stay underground as much as possible anyway. So it's mainly just me and the animals. And you, today. Lucky man."

"Happy to help." He eased his foot off the gas till they were barely moving. He grabbed her hand, which was still braced on the dashboard, and then squeezed it. "So, you're okay then?"

Her fingers warmed instantly, shooting a flare up her arm and into her heart. "Yeah, I'm okay. Mostly. But Nick, there's something I need to—"

A blatting sound to her right cut her off. Evie had caught up to them and the golf cart sat outside the passenger window. Hannah snatched her hand out of Nick's, even though she knew Evie couldn't see anything from below. Her expression must have given her away, though, because there was a sly grin on Evie's face.

"What's going on?" Evie called, directing the camera at them. "You're crawling along here like a couple of seniors on a Sunday drive."

Nick stopped the truck and leaned across Hannah to stare out the window. "Can you give us a little privacy?"

The camera swung left, and then right. "That's not what the show's about, brother. Our viewers want access to the princess. Privacy is bad for ratings."

Hannah rolled her eyes and laughed. "Never mind. This princess has had enough excitement for one day. I call CUT."

CHAPTER NINETEEN

Perching on the base of the bronze German shepherd in Bellington Square, Hannah asked, "Can we go home soon? I thought people voted for more time with the alpaca."

Evie was a proponent of constant viewer polling. Although fans of the show were interested in the pig, they were far more taken by the alpaca. There was no question that Alvina was adorable, with her plush brown and white coat, and now her lively personality was starting to show. She cavorted around the pen, kicking up her heels and coming to an abrupt stop in front of Evie's camera. The alpaca played to the crowd better than Hannah ever could.

Zooming out on the dog, Evie panned the camera around Bellington Square and the glittering gold brick of City Hall.

"It's important to ground the show in Dorset Hills," she said. "We want people to see exactly what the City looks like and stands for." She captured dozens of citizens going about their day with dogs on leashes. "Then we need to get the mayor on camera to back it up with words."

"Mayor Bradshaw?" Hannah's voice was shrill.

"None other. We have an appointment with him in 10 minutes."

Swallowing hard, Hannah croaked, "Why am I only hearing about this now?"

Evie looked over the camera at her. "Because I didn't want you to panic."

"Newsflash: I'm panicking."

"A little panic is good. Keeps you sharp." Evie beckoned. "Let's shoot you going up the stairs and through the doors. In fact, I'll stay behind all the way to his suite. We want to juxtapose the opulence against the farm's grittiness."

"I don't look like a princess today," Hannah said, clomping up the stairs in work boots, jeans and the purple checkered lumberjacket that had pretty much become her uniform. "The mayor almost ran over me last time he left you know."

"I wish I'd caught that," Evie said, following. "There's nothing more damning than a downed princess."

"Funny, Evie." She picked up speed a little, remembering the first time she'd visited City Hall. The mayor had treated her as a special guest—wooed her in fact. Her wealth had meant a lot to him then. Someone must have a much deeper wallet than hers to turn his head so quickly. She wondered what developer he was waltzing with now. No one had approached her directly to buy her land, so the City must be pulling the strings.

"Can you slow down?" Evie said. "It's not easy to keep you in focus when you're practically running. But I love the intensity."

Hannah opened the doors of the mayor's suite and walked into reception. The young woman behind the desk yanked out her earbuds and said, "Oh. Hi, Evie. Is the mayor expecting this?"

"Hey Chloe. He is, yes. Can you tell him I'm here?"

Chloe fluffed her hair for the camera and then covered the receiver as she spoke to the mayor. "He's—uh—been detained," she said, putting the phone down.

"No problem," Evie said, gesturing for Hannah to sit down in one of the guest chairs. "We'll wait."

Chloe cleared her throat. "It might be better to come back when he has more time."

"Really?" Evie lowered the camera. "Well, if you think that's best. Hannah had something to give him."

Hannah got up and followed her out, surprised Evie would give up that easily. But Evie just led her a few yards down the long hallway and into the alcove that led to the ladies' room.

"What are we—?"

"Hush. Just give it a second," Evie whispered. "He won't be able to resist coming out to see what you've got for him."

Sure enough, the old oak door creaked open and footsteps came toward them. Evie held up her fingers: five, four, three, two and—

Hannah stepped out into the main corridor and Mayor Bradshaw leapt backwards on his expensive loafers. He was elegant and nimble even when escaping the spotlight he usually sought. "Hannah," he said. "How lovely to see you. What brings you to City Hall?"

"First, I wanted to return your ring, sir. I rented a metal detector to find it. But on top of that, I'm touring the town for my new online series. We've visited a dozen dog bronzes and wanted to get a statement from you."

"A statement? About what?"

Hannah gave him her sweetest smile. "About your mission here in Dog Town. That's all. My fans will want to hear it directly from your lips."

His sharp eyes narrowed. "This really isn't a good time. I was about to get on Skype with my spiritual guru."

Evie lowered the camera and smiled at him. "Sounds great, sir. We'd love to catch that."

"Evelyn, really. I offered you a job as my chief of staff. Now you're running around shooting a reality TV show that's not even on TV? You had talent and I'd hoped for better for you."

"Don't give up on me yet, sir," Evie said, grinning. "I thought a lot about how I could spread the word about Dog Town to the world. You've got to go where the people are, and these days, that's online. Honestly, though, I was shocked at how quickly we gained a following."

He rolled his eyes. "For The Princess and the Pig, I believe?"

"People are eating it up, sir. They love watching Hannah's trials and tribulations as she adapts to country living after the big city."

"It's like a modern Green Acres and just as silly," he said. "I don't suppose you're old enough to remember that show."

"Exactly!" Evie said. "It's Green Acres for the reality TV age. And honestly, there's never been a better time to reach people directly. We've had countless questions about Dorset Hills after just four episodes. I was hoping to feature a regular 'Ask the Mayor' segment."

He backed up, holding up his hand. "I'll need to check in with my new PR person. Your post didn't stay empty long, Evelyn."

"As your former PR person—the one you wanted to

promote—I think it's the perfect platform for telling all of North America about the magic of Dog Town. In fact, our audience is global. Think about the opportunity."

With his back against the oak door of his suite, he said, "We don't have housing to accommodate an influx of dog-lovers, unfortunately. With land at such a premium, we may need to hang out our 'Full' sign."

"We'll never be too full for tourism dollars. Our Canadian fan base is growing by leaps and bounds and they do love their bus tours. Dog Town businesses will thrive like never before."

"I don't think so, Evelyn." He opened the door, slipped through it and said, "But it was lovely to see you."

"We're meeting later this week about my plan to create a service dog center," Evie said. "Don't forget."

"Check in with Chloe and reconfirm, would you? It's such a busy time." Closing the door, he added, "Have a good day, ladies."

"Sir, your ring?" Hannah called.

"Keep it," he said before the door clicked shut. "As a memento."

Evie handed the camera to Hannah as they walked out of City Hall and down the front stairs.

"Well, that was a bust," Hannah said.

Evie turned so fast that ginger curls blocked her eyes. "Are you kidding? We got the mayor on camera basically thumbing his nose at local businesses. That's the kind of thing that turns tides, Hannah."

"I've never really understood politics, I guess," Hannah said, slapping the big bronze German shepherd with her free hand as they passed.

"That's why you have me, my friend." Evie looked over her shoulder at City Hall and smiled. "I thought I knew the place well when I worked here. But after getting knocked on the head, I see so much better."

"It's enough for me to know you think we're winning," Hannah said.

Evie took the camera back. "Stick with me, Princess. I'm going to make your farm famous."

"HUH. MY BROTHER'S HERE. AGAIN." Evie pulled her car up beside his truck. "He must have missed me more than I imagined."

"Twin power, I guess," Hannah said. "I've been trying to get James to visit ever since I bought this place and it hasn't worked yet."

"You've told him about the show, right?" Evie asked.

Since the camera wasn't rolling, Hannah made a face. "Are you kidding? He'd be appalled. I just said we needed to be creative about getting the mayor's attention. He was surprised the mayor wasn't listening. James is sentimental about Dorset Hills. He won't hear a bad thing about it."

"Give it time. Embracing the good and the bad about this town is the only way to survive."

"Speaking of good and bad," Charlie said, joining them. "I have news."

Evie's camera shot up instantly. "Rolling."

"I don't recall signing a waiver for this," Charlie said, but he turned his head a little to the right, perhaps to show his best side.

"Right. Waivers," Evie said. "Good point, Charlie. I've got yours in my car. Anyway, give us the bad news first."

He looked at Hannah and she nodded. "Someone dumped a llama in the bush behind the barn. Tied it to a tree, in fact. I heard the poor thing bleating and went to collect it."

Rubbing her eyes, Hannah sighed. "And the good news?"

"The good news is that the alpaca needed a buddy and the llama will fit the bill. Once he's out of isolation, I'll introduce them."

"They won't, uh, mingle the wrong way?" Hannah asked.

Charlie laughed. "They can and they might. We'll need to get the vet out to castrate the newcomer. When Wilma's delivered, we'll have her done, too. Otherwise, this place will be overrun."

"It'll be overrun anyway, with people dumping their livestock. Where are they coming from? They mayor said livestock isn't permitted in Dorset Hills. Are people crossing county lines?"

Charlie shrugged. "I wouldn't want to speculate, but people obviously know a good opportunity when they see it. This critter won't be the last, I wager."

Turning to face the camera, Hannah said, "People, Runaway Farm is a small hobby farm. We can't keep adding any animal that comes along. As Charlie here has explained to me, there's an art to livestock management. If you want your animals to be happy and healthy, you need to run a tight ship. So please, say no to dumping."

"On the bright side," Charlie cut in, "we have a very happy alpaca. A smart, trainable alpaca, actually. The curtain's rising out back now on her first show."

"Bring it on," Evie said, moving ahead as they walked to the alpaca's pasture.

On the long side of the fence, Alvina was facing Nick, making a happy, humming sound. He clapped his hands to get her full attention, and said, "Ready?" Then he started singing an old song in a surprisingly nice voice: "You Make Me Feel Like Dancing."

His voice got breathy as he ran down the outside of the fence. Alvina kept pace on the inside. When they reached the far end, he started back. This time he did an odd silly prance, waving his arms and hopping. Inside, Alvina hopped, spun in a circle, bucked and kicked up her heels.

Back and forth they went, with Nick's moves getting more elaborate and Alvina responding enthusiastically. Hannah leaned against the fence, laughing helplessly.

Meanwhile, the camera bobbed left and right, up and down, as Evie caught every nuance of her brother's strange dance. When she lowered the camera, her smile faltered. "Poor guy," she muttered. "Nick's got it bad for this girl."

CHAPTER TWENTY

The young limo driver who'd dropped Hannah off five weeks ago smirked as he pulled up in front of the porch. "Good morning, ma'am," he said.

"Back at you, fine sir," she said, smiling.

"Am I missing an inside joke?" A tall, dark man got out of the opposite side of the limo, grinning. His eyes were light, clear blue and his teeth were white.

"You had to be there, sir," the driver said, accepting the bills James Pemberton pressed into his hand. "Oh wow. That's a lot. Your sister—"

"Careful," James said. "I'm one heck of a nice guy... unless someone disses my little sister. Even if she's a stingy tipper."

Hannah ran down the last few steps and hugged him. "I am far from stingy. But it does seem like my money doesn't go as far these days."

The driver left, and James crooked his arm around her neck. "Let's not waste a moment. I'm dying to see the suburban plot of land that has the nation up in arms."

"You're exaggerating," she said, leading him to the barn.

"I learned about The Princess and the Pig from my assistant in Paris. You've got some reach with that show, I'll give you that. People were talking about it even before they knew about my relationship with the rising star."

"Yet Mayor Bradshaw still hasn't folded," she said, beginning the tour, as usual, with the blind horse, Florence. "So the show must go on."

James scratched the mare's nose, ignoring the hair and dust already accumulating on his navy suit. In the past year, he'd begun working with their father, much to Hannah's dismay. They'd been more or less estranged from their father since before their mother's passing. It felt like a betrayal when James had taken a role in the import–export company. Worse, he'd left New York to work in various cities in Europe over the past nine months. Looking at him now, she had to admit he looked happy and healthy. Working hard seemed to agree with him in a way living in idle luxury had not.

Perhaps he would say the same about her one day, but given the way he was eying her battered boots and lumber jacket, it might take some convincing.

"Hannah," he said, peering in at the ewe, with her new lamb, "I don't understand all of this. The farm, and especially the show. I'm... worried about you."

She smiled. "You think I'm having some sort of breakdown, don't you?"

He took the barn in with a wave. "Well, come on. Sheep?" He looked out the double rear doors. "Goats?"

"That's not the worst of it," she said. "Someone dumped an ostrich on us yesterday. They came in the night and unloaded it with the pig. You never put new livestock in with your regulars, in case there's disease."

His blue eyes settled on hers. They were so like her

father's, whereas she'd inherited her mother's hazel. "Who stole my artsy-fartsy sister and replaced her with livestock lady?"

She leaned over and stroked the newborn lamb. "Have you ever watched a lamb being born?"

Her brother snorted. "They're hard to come by in New York. Or Paris, or Milan for that matter."

"Well, you don't know what you're missing. It was a minor miracle." She led him to the henhouse. "Every day I collect eggs. And each one of those is a miracle, too."

"Hannah." He held her back before she went inside. "Seriously. This is weird. What's gotten into you?"

She stopped and looked up at him. He didn't understand, but she could tell he wanted to. They'd gotten close after their mother's passing, and for years, she'd considered him her best friend. Although she didn't love him any less today, her world had expanded.

Looking around, she made sure they were alone. Charlie had gone to buy feed. And Evie had left for her daily visit with Roberto, her cat. For the past week, she'd been spending the night at Runaway Farm to make sure she didn't miss anything show-worthy.

Leading James out to the pig pen, she introduced him to Wilma. Picking up the scratching stick, she started running it over the pig's back. Her contented grunts made Hannah feel a little calmer.

"It all started a few months ago," she said, keeping her eyes on the pig to avoid seeing his expression. "Before I even knew about Runaway Farm." She tried to figure out a good lead-up and finally just blurted, "I'm pregnant."

James turned and stared at her profile. "You mean, with child? Or with pig?"

She gave a nervous laugh. "Both actually. Wilma's

expected to have more babies, sooner. If all goes well, I'll have a child around Christmas."

James was completely silent, which was unusual for her chatty brother. "Are you pulling my leg?"

"No. You're going to be an uncle, Jay." She started scratching the pig again. "If it works out, I mean. I'm almost three months, so I'm a little more confident that it'll actually happen." Finally she met his eyes. "If it's a girl, I'll call her Mavis, after Mom. May for short."

His eyelids seemed permanently locked in the open position. "Well. Shouldn't we crack some champagne?"

"It's 10 a.m. and I can't drink anyway," she said. "I've only stopped barfing the past few days."

Now he closed his eyes briefly. "I don't need to know the gory details—about that, or about farming." Pulling her into a hug, he said, "It's enough to know you're happy."

"I am," she said. "I'm scared though. Will you help me?"

"I'm with you every step of the way, sis. Even if I have to dodge around cow flaps to be here for you."

She sighed, relaxing a little for the first time since she'd passed under the arching sign over Runaway Farm. Community was a wonderful thing, but a big brother was a bonus.

"Thank you," he said, patting her shoulder.

"For what?"

"For not making me learn this online."

"Only two other people know," she said. "Remi and Mim Gardiner, a nurse. Charlie suspects, but he had the decency not to press for confirmation."

"My lips are sealed," James said, as Evie pulled into the parking lot. "Honestly, the less you say on this show the better, Hannah. You may live to regret this project."

"I may live to regret a lot of things," she said, leading

him to the fence bordering the alpaca's pasture. Alvina ran over, kicking up her heels and humming happily. "But you only live once, right?"

He stepped into a muddy pothole with his fine leather shoes. "You really call this living?"

"Try it, you might like it."

He took off his suit jacket and handed it to her. Then he bowed to the alpaca with a flourish. "I've admired your work, Alvina. Would you care to dance?"

EVIE DROVE them into town later that day. The mayor's office had called to invite Hannah and James for a meeting at City Hall. Chloe, the receptionist, had made it clear that Evie and her camera were unwelcome, but that didn't deter her one bit. The Pembertons needed a ride, and she was happy to oblige.

Mayor Bradshaw kept them waiting so long that James got up and started pacing in the small waiting area. Chloe picked up the phone and finally the mayor's door opened and he welcomed them inside, giving James' hand a hearty shake and ignoring Hannah's completely.

Creeping through the door right behind them, Evie caught the handshake diss on camera.

"Evelyn," the mayor said. "This is a private meeting with the Pembertons. You were not invited."

"She's an honorary Pemberton now," Hannah said, smiling. "It's a shame she got so injured in the line of civic duty, but your loss is my gain. I don't know how I'd manage without her now."

"I'm barely over my concussion," Evie said. "But I was happy to take a hit for Dorset Hills."

Moving behind his desk, he gestured to the two leather seats situated in front of it, leaving Evie to stand.

"Head injuries can leave lasting damage," he said. "Perhaps that explains why you don't seem to be on side with the City anymore, Evelyn."

"On the contrary, sir. Hannah's show has attracted so much positive attention. We went around yesterday to interview local businesses and she was practically swarmed. The *Dorset Hills Expositor* came out and interviewed her."

He sat behind his big oak desk and smiled. "I quashed that story. Or at least, postponed it. I have doubts about whether your little production is presenting Dorset Hills in the right light."

Hannah finally spoke. "I thought any publicity was good publicity."

"Hardly." He withered her with a stare. "We have a certain gravitas in Dorset Hills—an image to uphold. It doesn't align with The Princess and the Pig, I'm afraid." Turning to James, he added, "I suspect your brother would agree with me."

James offered a bland smile. "I back my sister in every project she takes on, Bill."

The mayor flinched slightly at the casual use of his name. "As one businessman to another, I'm sure you realize this so-called show doesn't align with *your* current business interests, either. You're probably losing clients because of it."

"Perhaps." James shrugged. "Our father's company has faced worse than a dancing alpaca." He looked at Hannah. "Some clients called after you posted a preview of my dance with Alvina. It was a bigger hit than I expected."

"You can never go wrong dancing with an alpaca,"

Hannah said. "Mom would have been proud of your courage."

James reached over and squeezed her arm. "She'd be even prouder of you, Hannah. You're the brave one."

The mayor cleared his throat. "This is touching, but I was hoping we could have an adult conversation."

Hannah smiled. "I can't remember my brother and I having a more mature discussion. We've turned a corner in our relationship."

"Lovely," the mayor said, picking up his phone and tapping. "Let me know when this private moment is over." Lowering the phone, he glared at Evie. "I didn't grant permission for you to film."

"I'll make the town look good, sir. I always do."

James leaned forward and rested his hands on the mayor's desk. "Bill, why are we here? Hannah's got farm chores lined up for me and I could really use the exercise."

Color rose in the mayor's tanned cheeks. "Then I'll get straight to the point." He looked at Evie. "Out."

Evie sighed. "Okay, but then I'll only hear Hannah's side. Why not speak your piece directly, sir?"

"Don't make me call security." He jerked his thumb at the door. "As for your plans for a service dog center... I wouldn't hold your breath, Evelyn."

After she left, the mayor said, "James, a very significant developer wants to build on the land your sister now owns."

"Oh? And how does she feel about that?"

Hannah leaned forward and put her hands on the desk, mimicking James' position. "There's hardly enough land to interest a significant developer. What aren't you telling me, Mayor?"

"We're in discussions with Wolff County to make some adjustments," he said. "That's all I'm at liberty to say. But with the money you'd make from the deal, you could relocate your menagerie anywhere you like."

"I made Bob Hess a deathbed promise that I'd keep the farm intact, and I don't take commitments lightly, Mayor."

"Bob's primary interest was keeping his animals safe and happy. We could find you a new location with even more land."

James turned to Hannah. "It may be worth considering, as long as the City promised to stop breathing down your neck." He looked at the mayor. "Would you stand down on the harassment, Bill?"

The mayor winced again. "I would hardly consider my few house calls harassment."

"You've changed policies so many times I can barely leave my farm without a passport," Hannah said.

"It would be more peaceful," James said to Hannah. "That counts for something."

"It does. But I made a promise to Bob to keep Runaway Farm safe." She smiled at the mayor. "I appreciate your offer, but I'm going to have to decline."

He sat back in the chair and crossed his arms. "Don't make me play hardball, Hannah."

Hannah looked at James. "Care to translate? Since this is meant to be a man-to-man discussion?"

"Are you threatening my sister, Bill?" James asked. "I don't take kindly to that."

"Of course not," the mayor said. "I'm just concerned about the new addition to your family. I assumed you'd want to keep things peaceful, like you said."

Hannah felt the color drain from her face. "New addition? You mean the ostrich?"

Mayor Bradshaw laughed for the first time. It wasn't a pleasant sound. "I've heard from a reliable source that you're going to be an uncle, James. I know you'll want the best for the little tyke, and the wrong side of the city is no place to raise a child."

Hannah's mind spun furiously as she pondered how he could have heard about her pregnancy. If it wasn't Charlie, the only likely leak was at the hospital, where Remi had mentioned the baby. What if the curtains really did have ears? Fox Spinner had been there that day, with her injured arm. Others may have heard, too.

James rose and leaned over the desk. "You *are* threatening us, Bill. That never ends well. It would force us to play hardball, too."

The mayor rose and the two men stood, face to face. Hannah circled around her brother and walked to the door.

"Excuse me, Mayor, but I've got a vet coming to see my new ostrich. Feel free to come by for a dance with the alpaca anytime. It would do you a world of good."

"Don't make offers you can't stand behind," he said, seeing them to the door. He closed it very firmly behind them.

CHAPTER TWENTY-ONE

Hannah burst into tears when she saw the empty pasture where Alvina had danced. Charlie was still offsite, and during that rare time when no one was on the premises, someone had snipped two locks and stolen the alpaca. There was no sign of her being taken by force, so it appeared she had passed through the gate willingly.

"It's the mayor," she said, wiping her face on the rough sleeve of her lumberjacket. "He texted someone while we were in his office and then made a vague threat about Alvina. He's playing hardball."

"The most obvious answer isn't always the correct one," Evie said.

James paced back and forth, clenching his hands into fists. "He's behind it, either directly or indirectly. He threatened Hannah in other ways, so why stop there? Taking out the most popular cast member is a good way to derail the show."

"If so, that's where he's wrong," Evie said. "Reality shows thrive on drama. This twist will increase ratings."

She turned on the camera and scanned the empty pen, and then zoomed in on Hannah's face.

"I don't care about ratings," Hannah said, blocking the shot with one hand. "I just want my alpaca back. Of all the animals, she's my favorite."

"It's hard not to like an alpaca," James said. "Mind you, she's the first I've ever met."

"Don't let Wilma hear that," Evie said. "Nick said you were plenty upset when she went missing."

Hannah sighed. "I'm just emotional these days. Animals really work their way into your heart."

"Well, look what happened with the pig," Evie said, filming again. "She came home. Prima found her. Maybe she could do the same with Alvina."

Hannah brightened. "Maybe. But Alvina despised Prima. The llama does, too. Their hatred of dogs is innate."

"That doesn't mean Prima can't find her. Maybe Leo, with his beagle nose, can help." She turned off the camera. "We need to call the Mafia."

Within the hour, the lime-green van pulled into the parking area, followed by a dozen other vehicles, including Sally's golf cart. Nick had picked up Remi and Leo along the way and the beagle's head hung out one window. Clive, Nick's golden retriever, peered out the other, tongue lolling.

Cori rallied everyone in the parking area. "We'll divide into teams," she said.

"I'll go east," Sally said. "I'm most familiar with that terrain. Duff, Maisie and Sasha, you're with me."

Cori raised her eyebrows. Normally she assigned teams, according to some system known only to her. This time she let it go. Sally was an experienced rescuer, and gray power probably held more sway than anyone else's.

The trainer assigned Hannah, James, Nick, Remi and Bridget to her team and they went south. Their team included Leo and Beau, Bridget's canine external hard drive.

The other teams dispersed north and west on foot. When they were out of sight, Cori said, "Let's go through the motions, although honestly, I can't imagine anyone getting that alpaca out of here without a truck."

Remi had taken Leo to the pen, and then walked him all over the parking area. His tail continued a steady wag but never picked up the pace, as it normally did when he was on a scent.

"I want to bring Prima along," Hannah said. "She found Wilma."

Cori shook her head. "Beau's a better bet, and he hates Prima."

"He doesn't hate Prima," Bridget said, resting her hand on the tall dog's head. "He just finds her energy a bit much."

"We can try Prima later," Cori said. "For now we need the best dog power we've got."

"Let's go," Remi said. "Every hour means the scent fades."

"And the light," Evie said, joining them with her camera.

Cori rolled her eyes. "I don't recall picking you for my team."

"I go where Hannah goes," Evie said. "This alpaca abduction is very likely a political move. Who best to combat that but me?"

Shrugging, Cori raised her index and flipping finger and pointed south. "Deploy."

FOUR HOURS LATER, two dozen weary people gathered in the wood-paneled living room of Runaway Farm. The search party had swelled through the evening and now sprawled over couches, chairs and the old shag carpet. Evie sat on the stairs and shot the discussion through the railings.

Duncan rode around on Hannah's shoulder, squawking his protests about the whole affair. Normally Hannah would be embarrassed over the nest the bird had created in the recliner's upholstery, but Nick had taken that seat so no one had noticed.

"Let's reconvene at first light," Cori said. "I'll sleep on the couch."

"I'll stay, too," Remi said.

A dozen other voices agreed, and James looked at Hannah with surprise. She gave him a smile, acknowledging the community that had sprung up around her here.

"I'll give up my bed," James said, looking at Kinney Butterfield. She had joined them late, but forged through the bush with a ferocity that left James trailing in her wake.

Of all the women there, Kinney would have been Hannah's guess as least likely to catch her charming brother's eye. Not that Kinney wasn't attractive; she was one of the prettiest women in a room full of lovely faces. But Kinney's expression was always serious, even to the point of sadness. James had always been drawn to the light, or so it seemed to Hannah. His girlfriends had mainly been angular blondes who played tennis and were perfectly manicured. She looked down at her own nails, all of them ragged and dirty, and realized she hadn't done her nails since she left New York. Her primping had dropped to the bare minimum required by Evie's camera.

"Let's order pizza," Remi said, "Although someone will need to go into town to pick it up."

"I'll do it," Kinney said. "I could use a drive."

"I'll come with you," James said. "I'd love a tour around town. I'll be staying a while, and so much has changed."

After they left, Evie caught Hannah's eye and beckoned her into the den. "We have a problem," she said.

"We most certainly do," Hannah agreed.

"Not the alpaca," Evie said. "Although that's certainly a problem. I've been online posting about it, and I'm sorry to say that a malicious rumor has started circulating about you. This kind of thing seems to be inevitable when you get bigger."

"What kind of rumor?" Hannah's throat was so tight it felt like she was forcing the words out one by one.

Evie's face flushed. "Someone posted that you're pregnant. It's the kind of lie that gains traction quickly, unfortunately."

"Ah," Hannah said. James wasn't around to speak for her, and she suddenly felt terribly alone. Remi arrived in the den as if on cue, and looped her arm through Hannah's.

"She doesn't look pregnant at all," Remi said. "Why would people say such a thing?"

Hannah took a deep breath. "Because it's true. The mayor knows it's true and apparently he'd sink low enough to use it."

"First... congratulations," Evie said. "I'm so happy for you. I can't say it hadn't crossed my mind, with you throwing up all the time."

"Yeah, I did drop that obvious hint." Hannah managed a faint smile. "But not on the mayor's watch. He said he heard it from a reliable source."

"The farm must have a mole," Evie said.

"Charlie?" Remi said. "I can't believe that. He only wants the best for you."

"People have different ideas of what's best sometimes," Evie said, staring at her phone. "To make things worse, they're questioning your values, having a child out of wedlock."

Hannah winced. "People still say things like that?"

"They do. Even here in Dog Town, which is a progressive town in many ways."

"Next they'll be speculating about the father," Remi said, sighing. "No one can resist that kind of mystery."

Pushing the curls away from her forehead, Evie looked up, but she couldn't quite meet Hannah's eyes. "Already happening."

"Oh no." Scooping up Prima, Hannah buried her face in the dog's fur. "Who are they targeting?"

"Me." The deep voice startled her, and she turned to see Nick standing in the doorway, holding up his phone. "Looks like I'm the last to know I'm the baby daddy."

His tone was light enough but his face had flooded with color up to his auburn hairline. He pressed his lips together as if to stop himself from saying more.

Hannah walked toward him, with Prima in her arms. The dog air snapped in Nick's general direction, and he stepped back, jerking his sleeve out of reach.

"I'm sorry, Nick," Hannah said.

"I'm used to her," he said. "I don't think she actually wants to bite me."

"No, I mean I'm sorry about... the other thing. The gossip. It's what I was trying to tell you the other day."

Nick held up his hand, palm toward her. "You don't owe me—or anyone else—an explanation, Hannah. I just..." He turned quickly to leave. "Congratulations."

CHAPTER TWENTY-TWO

"You guys never showed me this one," Hannah said, catching sight of the bronze pricked ears of a statue looming over the scrub at the base of the old trail. They'd driven to the less popular end of the hill system and a trail the City never advertised.

"I didn't know about it either," Evie said. She looked almost naked without her ever-present camera, but Cori had threatened a slow, painful death to anyone who disclosed the location for their top-secret Mafia meetings.

"Vow of silence," Remi said, as they started up the trail. "Cori would probably stake us out on the statue and let vultures pick at us. Like Zeus did to Prometheus."

"I like the way you think," Cori said, coming up the trail behind them. Dressed all in black, she moved like a stealthy panther. Sticks and leaves didn't crackle under her feet as they did the others. "I hate desecrating this spot with outsider energy. This is where we get our best ideas."

Hannah could understand why the Mafia had chosen this small clearing as their official meeting place. The massive bronze chow chow was not only isolated in the bush, but also just as menacing as the German shepherd in Bellington Square. It looked like a fluffy wolf ready to devour wayward rescuers.

Evie was staring around, recording the scene in her mind, if not on camera. "Thanks for allowing us in. I'll never breathe a word of this, I promise."

"You'd better not," Cori said. "I see you clocking every detail, Evie Springdale. There's something different about you since your concussion."

"Near-death experiences have a way of clarifying things," Evie said. "I got smarter after that bonk on the head."

"Mind games," Cori said, orange finger flashing as she tapped her own head. "From what's left of your mind. Just forget about this place, you two. Invitation only."

"I'd never find it again anyway," Hannah said. "Even if I could drive."

Cori's lip twitched, but she caught the smile before it bloomed. "Maybe it's better to leave those lessons till you've delivered another human the world doesn't need."

"Cori!" Remi practically spit out the word. "Don't say things like that."

Remi rarely gave Cori the satisfaction of reacting anymore, so now the tiny trainer's smile did blossom, complete with pearly teeth and pointy fangs.

"What?" Cori said. "Everyone knows the world's over-populated, not just Dog Town. Why Hannah would be in a rush to add another is beyond me."

"Her reasons are none of your business," Remi said. "And she's probably not the only one of us hoping to add to Dog Town's population."

Ahead of them, Sasha raised her hand. She was sitting on the base of the statue, wearing a black baseball cap over her blonde hair. "I am. Half a dozen if I can pull it off."

"Me too," Nika said. "Three girls, three boys."

"That's more than your average litter of pups," Cori said. "Why can't you guys settle for rescue dogs? There are so many in need."

Bridget was almost invisible, leaning against a tree trunk in a khaki jacket. "It doesn't push the same buttons, my friend."

Cori's grinned vanished completely. "Not you, Bee. I thought you were above such primitive urges."

"I'm as human as the rest of you," Bridget said, shoving herself off the tree. "I see no reason why we can't fill our homes with kids *and* dogs."

"And cats," Evie said. "Roberto's my trial run at childrearing. If I can keep him alive, I'll go bigger."

Hannah cleared her throat. "I've got a barn full of responsibility. Somehow I need to figure out how to raise a human on top of all that."

"Right," Remi said. "That's why we're here. To discuss our impasse with the mayor."

"I hate to say it, but I think he's won this battle," Sasha said.

Duff joined them in time to hear the last comments. "That doesn't mean he's won the war."

"Far from it," Evie said, shoving her hands into her pockets, as if she no longer knew what to do with them. "He thinks he's outplayed our 'politics by public relations' strategy. But I've got a few moves left."

"What are you thinking?" Bridget asked.

"First, we need to figure out where he's stashed the alpaca." Evie looked around at the group. "How hard can it be? You guys have connections all over town. Alvina's a big animal, and now she's practically a household name."

Another shape emerged from the shadows. Kinney Butterfield had been as still as a statue herself. "I've been talking to my contacts inside government and they seem genuinely surprised about the alpaca. I'm not sure the mayor's behind that move, to be honest."

"He's got to be," Cori said. "Who else would have the motivation or means? It's no small feat to steal a 180-pound animal."

"Quickly, too," Hannah said. "We were only in town for two hours. Charlie was decoyed into town on what seemed to be a bogus call. The special supplements he ordered weren't there when he got to the holistic pet store. No one knew what he was talking about."

Evie stared up at the chow chow. "You're sure Charlie's one of the good guys, right?"

A chorus of voices sang out a resounding "yes."

"We've known him a lot longer than you," Cori pointed out.

"Yeah, but people change. Sometimes you get hit in the head and it *doesn't* make you smarter."

Cori sighed. "That's why we checked out Charlie's house. And Fox Spinner's house too, if you must know. I hated to do it, but you're right, sometimes people turn if the motivation is high enough."

Evie signaled Nika and Maisie to ask for a boost. They cupped their hands and, stepping into them, she hoisted herself onto the chow chow's back. After sliding around for a second on the smooth bronze, she steadied herself.

"What do you see?" Hannah asked, wishing she could climb up, too. Sitting atop fierce dog statues was probably off limits forever. Even after the baby came, she'd have to be more careful than most, especially around a farm. For a moment, the thought of being a single mom felt like a responsibility as heavy as a bronze sculpture.

"I see a town that pretends to be inclusive, but is surprisingly small-minded," Evie said, staring over the hills to the quaint city below. "And I see Runaway Farm at the very edge of all that... pushing the boundaries."

"The town's not that bad," Remi said. "I've lived here all my life and there are some wonderful people, both old school and new. It's like most places, I guess. But the spotlight you've shone on the town is showing the dark corners."

"No one looks perfect under a spotlight," Duff agreed.

Bridget's fingers rested on Beau's head as always, perhaps drawing wisdom by way of the quiet, dignified dog. "I think Evie's right," she said. "We know Bill Bradshaw's ways. It's not that he wouldn't steal an alpaca if he could. I just think it's a little beyond his skill set. His people bumble enough with dogs, let alone livestock."

"He told me he'd hired good help," Evie said. "I don't think they're all on the public payroll."

"Still, it would take an expert to kidnap an alpaca. They're flighty, sensitive creatures," Hannah said. "I worry about Alvina. We were just getting her settled."

"We'll get her back," Bridget said. "If there's one thing we've learned in rescue it's that garbage floats to the surface eventually. You have to poke around the swamp a little and let the current swirl it up."

"We don't have that kind of time," Hannah said. "Alvina won't fare well in some dark shed alone. She needs companionship."

Evie swung her leg over until she was sitting sideways on the statue and holding a bronze ear tight. "I know the mayor would sink low enough to expose Hannah's secret and derail the show. But I get the sense he didn't put that train in motion. Oddly enough, he's often the follower and not the leader."

Hannah stared up at her. "If he's not leading the fight against me and Runaway Farm... who is?"

"Someone's probably feeding him information to get something in return," Bridget said. "That's how it usually works."

"I've got an idea," Evie said. "It'll take guts, Hannah. You've got a huge platform now and they're waiting for your response. You can grab the bronze dog by the ears and meet it head on." She let go of the chow and slid down its sleek side to land lightly among them. "But no one could blame you for walking away at this point."

"I'd blame her," Cori said. "She made a commitment. That means something."

"She made a commitment to Bob before she knew she was expecting a baby," Remi said. "And I feel guilty for roping her into it. Now she has to think about raising a family in Dorset Hills."

Hannah sat down on the base of the statue. "James is so angry. He wants me to move back to New York."

"He's angry about the baby?" Remi asked.

"No, not that," Hannah said quickly. "He's excited about being an uncle. He just thinks the environment here has become toxic."

"He's not wrong," Duff said. "It's getting harder and harder to breathe around here. Hannah, you need to do what's best for your family."

"What do *you* want?" Remi asked, squatting beside Hannah to meet her eye to eye.

"I... I'm not sure. A baby changes everything," Hannah

said. "It's not just about me thumbing my nose at the city anymore. I've got to think long term."

"Sticking it to the mayor *is* thinking long term," Cori said. "You're making Dog Town a better place for kids to grow up. What better motivation is there than that?" She smirked before adding, "Other than making it a better place for dogs, of course."

"All I wanted to do was move home and maybe build a little inn," Hannah said. "Why do I have to carry the torch for the cause?"

"Because you're the only one with a dancing alpaca," Cori said. "No one else can get that sort of attention at the moment."

"We all try to take our turns," Bridget said. "And one day we'll prevail against the rot growing in this city. If it's not today, that's okay. We'll get another chance."

Staring up at them, Hannah felt the chill of the granite platform through her jeans. They were giving her an out. She could throw down the torch and still keep them as friends, and it was terribly tempting. James' frustration and Nick's stony silence had taken a toll. Going back to the anonymity of the big city had a lot of appeal. In New York, no one expected anything of her, other than handouts. Here, she had to think, scheme and dance like an alpaca— all while nauseated.

But their faces... So many friendly faces. They wanted the best for her, and they wanted the best for their community, too. A community that she'd craved, and enjoyed briefly, before feeling the weight of "taking her turn."

"Okay," she said at last. "I'm not quite ready to let Bill Bradshaw drive me out of Dorset Hills."

"That's the spirit," Cori said, offering one gloved hand

to pull Hannah to her feet. "If we were recruiting for the Mafia, you'd be a contender."

"Really?" Hannah asked, brushing off her pants and smiling for the first time that day.

Cori rolled her eyes. "No, not really. You can't rescue animals in a golf cart. Or a limo, for that matter. A driver's licence is a prerequisite for Mafia work."

Walking ahead of her down the trail, Hannah flipped her the finger without looking back. "Mayor Bradshaw shouldn't underestimate me, Cori, and neither should you."

CHAPTER TWENTY-THREE

Sitting on the bleachers of Dorset Hills High School, Hannah felt oddly exposed in a pretty white sundress she'd worn dozens of times. Nowadays, she preferred the comfort of bibbed overalls, or at least jeans. But Evie had told her to look the part of the princess today, and she followed orders. At least she'd been able to bring Prima along. The dog had quickly become part of every outfit. If the terrier's small body wasn't under one arm, she actually felt chilly.

"And... rolling," Evie said, from her folding lawn chair directly in front of the bleachers.

"Hey everyone," Hannah said, hugging her dog, and giving the camera a weak smile. "Today this princess is taking a trip down memory lane... no pig included. You know where I ended up—on Runaway Farm—but you don't yet know how I got there. The story I tell you may be too much information for some of you, but given all the gossip that's been circulating, I wanted to clear the air. So, Prima and I are going to show you around *my* Dorset Hills."

Getting up, she walked backwards ahead of Evie, still

talking. "This is Dorset Hills High School, where I was pretty much your average teen. I sang in choir, waved some pom-poms on cheer squad, and got decidedly average grades. My brother, James, had been a superstar around here, and I always felt like I was in his shadow. On top of that, during my last year of high school, my mom and dad were fighting a lot. My brother was in college, Mom hid in her art studio and Dad turned into a workaholic. The only thing anyone agreed on was the dogs. In fact, I think they'd have divorced then if it weren't for our wolfhounds. We had three at that point, one for each of us, although my mom was queen." She held up Prima and the dog panted happily into the camera. "That's when I learned about the comfort dogs bring. It would take six of this terrier to equal a wolfhound in weight, but she's got more spirit and heart than any of them." She walked back to the bleachers. "This is where I met my first serious boyfriend. He was on the football team, and I thought I'd totally hit the jackpot. But wait till you hear what happened next."

"Cut!" Evie said, gathering her things. "That's great, Hannah. Do you want to take a break before the next scene?"

Hannah walked quickly to the parking lot. "Let's get it done before I lose my nerve."

Opening the trunk, Evie said, "I'm not sure this is such a good idea. Once this stuff is out there, you can't take it back."

"What they're saying isn't fair. I'm going to correct those misperceptions." She turned and smiled. "Thanks for giving me a platform to do it."

They drove in silence to the Larkson Grand hotel, and walked around the back to the manicured trails in the bushes. Hannah gave Evie the signal to roll and started walking backwards very slowly down the trail.

"Here's where my life changed forever," she told the camera, setting Prima on the ground and unhooking her leash. "Senior prom was wonderful. I wore this strapless dress my mom had picked out for me in New York City. It was one of a kind. I felt like a princess. There, I said it." She grinned at the camera and then stumbled over a tree root and fell hard on her butt. Signalling Evie to keep rolling, she said, "That's pretty much how it happened. My date brought me back here, behind the hotel, for a romantic walk. The moon was nearly full. I remember that, because we didn't have a flashlight. I hadn't had a drop of alcohol but I was madly in love, and that's as big an intoxicant as anything else, isn't it? Well, the trails were rougher then than they are now, but we kept walking. My date had his arm around me and I felt as if nothing could ever happen to me."

Prima frisked around Hannah as she sat on the trail, and finally curled up in her lap. Evie knelt a few yards away, waiting, and finally Hannah continued to speak.

"My prom date assaulted me not far from where I sit now. I stumbled and... that was it. I won't go into the gory details, because enough people in town know his name. He's long gone now, and there's no reason for his family to suffer for his sins, as the old saying goes. Suffice to say that nothing was ever the same after that. As far as I know, only my mom and one friend knew about what happened. I left Dorset Hills with my parents, went to college, and eventually my parents divorced. Turns out the glue holding them together hadn't been the dogs, but me. And then everything took a terrible turn for the worse. Hang tight."

Evie pulled Hannah upright, and Prima dropped to the ground. "I'm so sorry, Hannah. I had no idea."

"Soon everyone will know," Hannah said, as they headed back to the car. "I'm tired of holding all of this in. It eats away at you."

"I couldn't get a permit to shoot inside the Barton Gallery," Evie said, as they drove the few blocks to the art gallery. "We'll have to shoot outside."

"Like hell we will," Hannah said. "I donated half a million to this place in my mother's name. That gives me a lifetime pass."

Evie stuck her camera in her backpack and followed Hannah into the wing that housed an exhibit of Mavis Pemberton's whimsical art, most of it featuring dogs. They waited till a young couple left and then started shooting.

Hannah walked from one display to another, trailing fingers over glass and then along the edge of a framed water-color of wolfhounds lolling in a field.

"Like many of you, I expect, I had ups and downs with my mother. Back then, she was just Mom, not Mavis Pemberton, celebrated artist. In fact, I resented her for really coming into her own after she left my dad. Her leaving broke his heart and I think it broke hers, too. Neither remarried, I can tell you that." She leaned against a pillar. "I like to think they'd have found their way back to each other eventually. Call me a shameless romantic."

Bending, she scooped up Prima. "Time ran out for my mom before that could happen. I'm ashamed to say we weren't on the best of terms for a few years. After college, I went my own way, working for charitable causes while my parents each made a fortune separately. I was angry and bitter—still carrying the burden of what happened at prom. But then one day, I got a call from my mom: she was sick."

Hannah slid down the pillar and sat cross-legged on the floor, with Prima in her lap. Evie mirrored her pose a few yards away.

"I won't drag this out, either, because Evie is already crying. Aren't you, Evie?" The camera bobbed up and down. "But there's something I want you to know: my mom had a genetic form of cancer that affects only women, and she didn't know it until it was too late. We had two years together, for which I am eternally grateful. By the time she passed, neither one of us had any doubt about how we felt about each other. She had asked me again and again to be tested and I refused. I didn't want to know if I carried this gene... and I certainly didn't want her to worry about me. What was done was done. In fact, it took a few more years till I was ready to face that verdict."

Pushing herself back up the pillar, Hannah carried Prima with her as she walked to a large painting of herself as a baby.

"When I got my results, I knew I needed to press fast-forward on my life and my plans. There are tons of options now that my mom didn't have and I expect to stay healthy for a good long while. But you don't sit around waiting with this gene. I knew I wanted a family, and that I might not find my dream guy in time. So I got started on my own. My child will be loved, and will have a wonderful community here. That's the main reason I came home to Dorset Hills."

Setting Prima down, she hopped onto a display case, which wobbled dangerously before settling. Then Prima leaped easily into her arms again.

"As for Runaway Farm, it's no secret I bought the place to fulfill a dying man's request. I had zero interest in roughing it farm-style. But in just six weeks, I've come to love that place, and more importantly, those animals. Yes,

I'm hoping to have a human family before too long, but as far as I'm concerned, pets are family, too. I love each and every animal on that farm. As you might have guessed, I love Alvina the alpaca most of all, and she's still missing. If you'll recall, I told you that alpacas are herd animals and can actually die of loneliness. That's why it breaks my heart to think she's shut up somewhere pining. Lorenzo, the llama, is her new partner in crime. They need to be together."

After a little pause, she hugged Prima so hard the dog finally squirmed. Then she stared into the lens again. "All my life, I've been a private person. That's so over now. I've got mixed feelings about that, given what's been said about me this week. But this show's also given me a chance to do some good for animals. It's given me a chance to tell people about an insidious, life-changing disease. And now that I've shared my whole story with you, I have a favor to ask. Please... stop trolling me on the internet and leaving a trail my child could find one day. Instead use all that energy for good. Spread the word about Alvina the dancing alpaca. If you're within shouting distance of Dorset Hills, organize searches. Put up signs. Ask friends of friends who might know. It's not easy hiding an alpaca, so I'm pretty sure that if we all put our heads together, we can figure out where she is and bring her home." Hopping off the display, she came toward the camera. "Thank you for letting me come into your lives these recent weeks. You're welcome in mine, too."

Prima jumped out of Hannah's arms and ran over to jump into Evie's lap, as she sat crying on the floor. "You are the bravest person I ever met," Evie said, moving Prima and getting to her feet.

"Or the stupidest," Hannah said, smiling. "Clean it up and get it online before I chicken out."

"Won't take long to edit. You've become a pro." Evie sneezed a few times. "Prima's turning into a fine therapy dog, but she's still a hazard to allergy sufferers everywhere."

"Time for your allergy meds, my friend," Hannah said, just as a security guard walked into the exhibit. "Unless I'm much mistaken, Runaway Farm is about to get a lot hairier."

CHAPTER TWENTY-FOUR

The first knock on the door came just half an hour after the new episode of The Princess and the Pig went live. As the sun hung low over Runaway Farm, a family of six arrived to help search for Alvina. Behind their van, a dozen other cars lined up, waiting to park.

Evie was monitoring the online activity on her phone. "It's going over great, Hannah," she called. "Someone's formed a group called Alvina's Army."

Cori came out onto the porch, rubbing her gloved hands together until they crackled from static and actually set off sparks like tiny fireflies. "Finally," she said. "I've always wanted to command an army. It's good to stretch myself a little."

Sally Taylor zigzagged around a long lineup of vehicles in her golf cart. "Holy moly," she said, hopping out and coming up the stairs. "I knew your show would shake things up, but this is crazy."

Hannah paced nervously as Cori, Bridget and Sally literally corralled people into an empty pasture. "I didn't expect people to just show up like that. Especially this late in the day. What are we going to do?"

From the bottom of the stairs, Duff said, "Let Cori and the girls handle the crowds. I'll call Sasha, Kinney and the guys to help out as well. We'll figure out a game plan to search every inch of this town and beyond. Meanwhile, you and Evie should stay inside, and I'll handle the traffic at the door." She clicked back up the stairs. "I'm a liability at night in these heels."

Hannah wrung her hands, but they didn't stay empty long. Prima catapulted from the porch into her arms, leaving scratches in the fresh paint. As usual when the weight hit her in the chest, she automatically clutched the dog.

"Go on back inside," Duff said, still texting. "Put Duncan in his cage, no matter how much he curses. Charlie's on his way to keep tabs on the livestock, and Nika can help with that."

"Shouldn't I stay out here to greet people? They've come to help."

Duff shook her head, and her glossy bob shone a rich auburn in the setting sun. "You're a distraction. Better to keep people focused on the alpaca."

Evie pulled Hannah into the house. "Leave it in their capable hands. The Mafia is used to directing crowds. They'll deploy soon and keep us posted on how it's going."

It turned out that they didn't need to go far for information. The Dorset Hills TV station had sent reporters out to cover the event as soon as heavy traffic coming into town caught their eye.

"This is incredible," Evie said, as they watched things unfold from her laptop. "There's a big group trying to storm the Animal Services building. The cops are there."

"I hope it doesn't turn violent," Hannah said, pacing behind her. "There are way more people than I ever imagined."

"That's what you get for sending out an impassioned plea." Evie squeezed her arm, and smiled. "Relax. This is exactly the kind of thing that will pressure the mayor to act. If he knows anything about the alpaca's whereabouts, she will likely reappear randomly and suddenly, as if she dropped from the skies. And don't be surprised if he stops harassing you in general. This story will get covered far and wide—maybe even in New York City, since you've got ties there."

Hannah sat down hard on a kitchen chair. "I guess there's no turning back now."

"It's a one-way street." Evie grinned at her. "Kind of like being pregnant. Which reminds me... Have you eaten?"

"This week?" Hannah patted her turbulent tummy. "Not much."

"Hannah! No matter how crazy this gets, you need proper nutrition. I'm going to heat up some soup for you right now."

She knew better than to protest when Evie got a head of steam. "Okay. Lots of crackers, please. And some tea."

"Just keep me posted if anything exciting happens," Evie said, heading for the kitchen.

"Everything's exciting," Hannah called. "With all the bobbing lights, it's like Hallowe'en."

While sampling different newsfeeds on Evie's laptop, Hannah ended up clicking on footage of her driving lesson with Nick. He hadn't been back to the farm since hearing her news two days earlier. At least that she knew of. Maybe he was out on foot patrol in Cori's army now, or maybe he'd never speak to her again. Either way, it gave her comfort to watch from behind as he explained the finer points of driving a standard truck. "Neutral. Clutch. First gear. Ease off clutch. Ease on gas." Nick's voice was even and soothing, no matter how many times she stalled out his truck. He was amazingly patient, she realized now. His smile faded only briefly when she hit the mailbox, and then returned by the time he carried it to Sally's shed.

Evie hadn't turned the camera off when they'd gone inside. Instead, she continued shooting as Nick carried the mailbox to Sally's shed. He grumbled over his truck for a few minutes and Hannah felt the heat rise in her cheeks.

"Hannah will pay for it, you know that," Evie told her brother, directing the camera lens around outside the shed.

Hannah's fingers hovered, ready to click off. She was eavesdropping on a private conversation about her, but it was hard to look away.

"I don't want Hannah to pay for my truck," he said. "This show was *your* idea. She'd never have agreed to drive it if you hadn't railroaded her."

"True. You'd tried to get her into your truck on your own and failed, brother. I gave you an assist."

He turned and glared at her. "I don't need your help with women, Evie."

"Not normally," Evie agreed. The image went dark inside the shed, but Nick flicked the light on his phone. "You did with this one. So I scored you a chance to make an impression."

"With you in the back seat filming? That's the best you could do?"

The image bobbed as Evie laughed. "Well, that was too good to pass up."

"But now she's got motion sickness," he said.

He heaved the mailbox off his shoulder and set it gently on the wood floor of the shed. He lingered in that position and Hannah found herself staring at his butt in the image. She shook her head and refocused and by that time, the camera was panning across the shed floor.

"It'll pass quickly," Evie said. "Unless she comes out here. This shed stinks."

"Yeah. Like dung," he said, backing into the camera. "Let's go check on Hannah. I'm worried about her."

"Stop worrying and just let things unfold," she said, following him out.

"Says little Miss Pushy..." His voice got faint and the screen went black.

Hannah was still staring at the darkened screen when someone cleared her throat. Evie was standing in the doorway with a tray of steaming soup and tea.

"I'm sorry," Evie said. "You weren't supposed to see that."

"It's okay. I didn't mean to snoop."

Evie set the tray down. "Nick's got it bad for you. But I guess you noticed that."

Blinking a few times, Hannah shook her head. "I— I didn't really notice anything." Pushing the chair back, she stood up. "If you'll excuse me for a second, I think I'm going to be sick."

EVIE CALLED through the bathroom door. "Hannah. Are you okay in there?"

"Yeah, I'm okay." Hannah was sitting on the tile floor with her head against the cool porcelain bathtub, using her phone to do some research. "I'll be out in a couple of minutes. Could you do something for me?"

"Of course. What?"

"I want to order food for when the search is over. Dozens of people will come back here. We need to make sure to treat them well. Maybe set up a barbeque in the pasture. Could you and Duff call around and see what you can do?"

"If you want hundreds of people hanging around all night, that's one way to guarantee it."

"I just want people to know I appreciate them. Besides, I'm still hoping it's a victory celebration, with Alvina dancing in her pen."

"Me too, but it's going to be tough finding a caterer at this hour," Evie grumbled.

"You'll find something. You always do."

Hannah waited until the footsteps receded. Then she quietly slit the screen, and climbed onto the toilet and out the bathroom window. From there, it was easy enough to jump to the flat kitchen roof below and shimmy down the post holding the clothesline. All those years of yoga had finally paid off in practical terms.

Sprinting across the backyard, she climbed two fences without using a flashlight, and ended up in Wilma's pen. It felt great to be moving, but she was glad Charlie had put the pig inside early to keep her safe from legions of fans.

One more fence, a sprint through a recently mown hay field and she got where she needed to be.

The old red tractor squatted in the bushes as if deliberately avoiding notice from the people starting to gather once more in the farm's parking lot. Voices carried across the field —some angry, some excited... all loud.

Hannah just hoped they were loud enough.

She lit up her phone long enough to check her footing and climb up on the tractor. Once seated, she took another look at the controls. It was a standard transmission. Of course. Why would driving a tractor be easy?

Charlie was the only one who used the big machine, usually to carry around hay or dung in the front basket. She had counted on the key to be in transmission, and luckily, it was. People might steal a pig and an alpaca, but they apparently didn't bother with expensive vehicles.

After pressing one foot on the brake and making sure the vehicle was in neutral, she turned the key. The tractor's roar could most certainly be heard from afar, but she expected most people—including Charlie, she hoped—to be too distracted to notice. If all went as planned, the sound would soon fade into the distance.

Misfires would attract attention, however, so she needed to get the tractor moving the first time. Sucking in a deep breath, she adjusted the throttle. There was a momentary screech and then a lurch, and finally, the big wheels started turning. Google had not let her down.

"Don't stop, don't stop, don't stall," she murmured, chugging forward along the side of the field. The shadows of the trees loomed on her left, but she didn't dare move further into the field. Instead, she bumped along in darkness, hoping she wouldn't hit a log... or something breathing.

At the end of the field, she turned left into another field, out of sight of her own farm. By then she felt confident enough that the beast wouldn't buck her off, and pulled out her phone to get some light. Then she dared to press harder on the gas to cover ground more quickly. Passing another farm, she turned off the light. Then she hit a couple of nasty bumps and turned it back on again, clinging for dear life.

Finally, she cleared the last field, passed through a gate,

and pulled up behind a garage. When she cut the engine, her ears rang so loudly that she turned in a full circle to make sure nothing was thundering up behind her.

Then she dashed to the shed, hoping to make a swift and dramatic rescue.

CHAPTER TWENTY-FIVE

The door of the shed was ajar and one flash of her light showed her what she'd hope to find was not inside. However, the footage on Evie's laptop was correct. The hut had a familiar smell, and there was mud along the wall at pig level. Two weeks earlier, Wilma had spent some time in this shed, before Prima found her and brought her home. Hannah had guessed that Sally Taylor repeated the same maneuver with Alvina, but apparently her neighbor had upped her game after a terrier outsmarted her.

The garage and one ramshackle outbuilding were also empty. That left only the old farmhouse. Had Sally taken in a camelid housemate? If not, she'd stashed Alvina somewhere else, and this whole mission would be for nothing.

It couldn't be for nothing.

Taking the front stairs two at a time, she tried the door.

Locked.

There was a stone on the porch about the size of a large baseball that looked about right for hiding a key. When she tipped it, there was only dirt underneath.

It would be perfect for smashing a window, however, if she could just be certain Alvina was actually inside.

Pressing her ear to the door, she listened.

"Alvina," she called. Quietly at first, and then more insistently.

Finally she started singing the old Leo Sayer song that Nick had used whenever he danced with the alpaca.

"You make me feel like dancing ... gonna dance the night away."

Once more, and much louder and then again, she pressed her ear to the door.

Inside she heard a shuffle, clicks of hooves on the floor and the heartrending bleat of a solitary alpaca.

"I'm coming, girl. Hang on," she said, and then continued to sing.

Inside, the bleated turned into a steady humming sound. Alvina believed in her. Now she had to make good on her promise.

Turning, she grabbed the rock. If she broke the window in the door or even the living room window, there was a chance Alvina would be cut on the glass. So she went around the side of the house to the kitchen window. Sally was likely fastidious enough to block off the kitchen from livestock.

An old wheelbarrow sat near the back of the house. She pushed it over to the window, flipped it and climbed up. It was just high enough to get a good look in the kitchen. The doorway to the living room was completely blocked by two large, stacked dog crates. On the other side of the wire mesh, Alvina's eyes shone red in the beam of her light.

Gripping the rock, she banged on the glass and shielded her eyes as it shattered. She pulled the sleeves of her hoodie over her hands to smooth shards away from the frame with the rock. Inside, Alvina was shoving the metal crates hard enough to make them rattle. It wouldn't take much to knock over the barricade and then stampede over the glass.

"Stay," she hissed, as if the alpaca knew basic commands.

Then she dropped the rock into the kitchen and hoisted herself through the window.

Glass pierced the fabric of her hoodie and pricked her as she dropped into the kitchen, cursing.

"Hey little girl, you just stay there and stay quiet," she crooned, crossing the kitchen floor and starting to pull out drawers. There was no way the alpaca would follow her peacefully through the crowds and into her pen. She'd need a leash of some kind.

The drawers yielded nothing, but when she twirled, she saw a couple of fancy leashes from Sally's bichon, which was barking from upstairs where she'd likely trapped the dog to be safe. Hands shaking, she set her phone down and clipped the leashes together. Then she gently eased the dog crates aside. Alvina charged through the gap and promptly defecated from excitement in the middle of Sally's kitchen floor. As odd as the timing was, Hannah couldn't help laughing.

"Wish you'd held onto that," she said, looping the leashes around the alpaca's neck. "Should have done it on her pillow."

Suddenly light flooded the kitchen and the animal reeled and hopped, taking Hannah along with her at the end of the lead.

Sally Taylor had her right hand on the light switch. "Looks like you've gotten yourself in a mess, Hannah," she said, calmly.

Indeed. Hannah now had one sneaker planted firmly in

the middle of the alpaca poop. "That's a shame," she told Sally. "I wanted to leave all of it for you."

"What's a shame," Sally said, "Is that you won't be leaving at all."

"Interesting," Hannah said. "How on earth do you plan to keep us here?"

Sally thumped the floor with something heavy and metallic. A pitchfork.

Hannah's heart jumped straight to fourth gear, but she tried not to make any sudden moves that would startle Alvina. "Sally. Surely you know that my army will march over here shortly."

"What I know is that you crawled out of the bathroom window and did this whole commando thing that was quite entertaining from where I was watching from the barn. I talked Nika into joining Cori so that I could keep an eye on you." Leaning against the wall, she offered a grudging smile. "You actually got the tractor going. I didn't give you enough credit."

"I'm sure you didn't. Let's talk about it over tea when Cori gets here."

"Cori's got her hands full. And I'm quite sure you didn't let anyone know you were skulking off."

"Actually, I texted Evie right before I broke your window."

Sally shook her head. "You didn't. You had this whole hero movie playing out in your head. Leading the alpaca home, you could finally get the respect you crave."

The comment stung hard enough to make Hannah's eyes water. "Half right," she said. "I do crave respect. But I texted anyway. I'm pathetic, not stupid."

"You're pathetic *and* stupid," Sally said, lunging for the phone on the floor.

Hannah kicked the phone out of Sally's path... and directly into Alvina's. The alpaca was getting agitated from the raised voices, and she brought one foot down hard on the small screen. Now Sally wouldn't be able to confirm one way or another whether Hannah had texted. But Hannah's lifeline was also cut off.

"If there's anything you'd like to tell me, you'd better speak fast," Hannah said. "Because we don't have much time."

"The only thing I'd like to tell you is that if I never see another egg, it will be too soon. You and your endless egg deliveries. Get a real job, princess."

"I have a real job. I run a successful farm rescue and I have a popular TV show." Hannah pulled gently until the alpaca turned, and then eased backwards until she could hop up on the counter. "How about you, Sal? Your life must be pretty scrambled if you have to climb into bed with Bill Bradshaw."

"I never—" Sally sounded scandalized.

"Figure of speech. I just mean you've been feeding the mayor information. What's in it for you?"

Sally stared at her with eyes that seemed to have shrunk to the size of Wilma's, and held equal menace. "It's a good thing you're pretty and rich, Hannah, because there's not much going on in here." She tapped her forehead.

"Oh, come on, I'm not that pretty," Hannah said. "The baby is stealing my looks."

"Well, you're pretty full of yourself if you can't figure out the lay of the land."

Hannah crossed her legs in the lotus position, scratching Alvina's head to keep her calm. "Oh, I think I got it: you desperately want to sell your property to developers and no one will touch it with a 10-foot pole unless mine comes along with it."

That color drained out of Sally's flushed cheeks. "Get your ass off my counter."

"What's a little butt print on your laminate when there's manure on your floor?"

Sally slipped around the dog crates and came toward her. "Newsflash: it's not that little. Anyone watching your show could see it grow by the day. Of course, I figured out your secret long before that. You were heaving every time I saw you."

"You do make me sick," Hannah agreed.

"But then I had the good luck to overhear you and Remi talking about your baby at the hospital after I cut my finger staking this stupid alpaca in your driveway."

"Where the heck did you get an alpaca?" Hannah asked. "Or acorns in spring, for that matter?"

Sally shook her head. "The internet always provides, doesn't it? Even without bags of money. Mind you, I'd hoped to spend less, driving you out."

"When it didn't work, you teamed up with the mayor."

She was standing so close now that Hannah could feel her hot breath. "Unfortunately, strategy never was Bill's strong suit. Like you, he relies too much on money and looks."

"I've got something he doesn't," Hannah said.

"What's that?"

"Friends," Hannah said simply.

"That won't help you now," Sally said. "You're not leaving here until you agree to sell your land."

"Won't happen. Not now, not ever. I'd rather get a taste of your pitchfork."

Sally swung the weapon over her shoulder. "I was

raised on a real farm, Hannah, and I've butchered plenty of things in my time. How about I show you my skills with the alpaca, and you can decide after that?"

Terror flooded Hannah's limbs, but she forced a smile and said, "Let me get more comfortable before you start."

Rising smoothly and swiftly onto her knees, Hannah pushed up to a standing position on the counter. Then she dropped Alvina's leash and got ready to leap. In the split second of targeting, a small tawny blur of terrier raced around the crates, jumped and hit Sally square between the shoulder blades. The older woman lurched forward and fell.

All Hannah had to do now was land beside Sally and kneel on her back. But Sally still had a few moves left. She rolled and pushed Hannah backwards, sending the dog crates flying. There was skirmish of terrier, alpaca, and suddenly, flashing neon fingers.

Strong arms helped Hannah up from the floor. "Get Alvina," she said.

"Already booked my next dance," Nick said, catching her as she fainted.

CHAPTER TWENTY-SIX

When Aladdin crowed the next morning, Hannah ignored the call for the first time ever. The second she opened the door, she'd be swarmed with people wanting to help—either friends, or fans of the show. The house was silent but there was a palpable current of energy as the rooster alarm continued. Rolling over, she covered her head with a pillow. There were things to do, decisions to make and she couldn't ignore them indefinitely, but she could enjoy this one brief moment of solitude.

"Hussy. Hussy. Hussy."

She sighed and then laughed. That was Duncan's fallback whenever he was distressed, perhaps because it got a reaction. He hadn't been thrilled to bunk with her and Prima, but she didn't dare leave him in the living room without supervision. He didn't like strangers, or blonde women or... anyone but her, really. The last thing she needed was anyone complaining to animal services about a bird attack. Especially when she'd been summoned to City Hall later.

Still in her pajamas, she headed into the hall, only to be caught in the lens.

"Morning," Evie said, zooming in. "I wanted to get some 'before' shots. Hope you don't feel as bad as you look."

"Evie, seriously. I almost got myself killed with a pitchfork last night."

"I know, and if you'd had the decency to text me even five minutes earlier, I could have had the camera with me. I missed filming Alvina spitting in Sally's face. What a moment!"

Hannah smiled. "I was out cold at that point. Which brings me back to requesting the day off."

"Day off? Are you kidding? This is the day the mayor backs down, fully and completely. We need to capture every moment."

"You don't know the mayor will back down."

Evie lowered the camera. "I do. It won't look exactly like backing down, but when you think about it later, you'll recognize it was a retreat. And my footage will document that beautiful moment for posterity."

Heading for the bathroom, Hannah said, "I'd better take a shower then. And think about what I want to wear for posterity."

"Think hard. You owe it to your fans to look good. They've worked hard for this moment."

"True. I hope you're feeding them breakfast."

Evie laughed. "I already got some shots of Nick in an apron scrambling eggs. It's one of the few things he can actually cook." She waggled her eyebrows. "In case you were wondering."

"Still matchmaking?" Hannah said, closing the bathroom door in Evie's face. "You're incorrigible."

"Interesting. The root of that word is 'Cori,'" Evie said,

through the door. "And speaking of our incorrigible friend, she's out reeducating Charlie on farm protocol and security. I've never seen her so rattled. She takes her recommendations very seriously, and Sally was someone she trusted."

"I don't blame Cori. Sally's the worst kind of adversary —she passed as a normal animal lover. My intuition about people is usually pretty good, too. Especially for money-hungry sneaks. Yet I didn't get a whiff of desperation off Sally. She never let on she was down to her last few dollars. That's why she sold her car."

"I'm just glad you're all right," Evie said. "I should have noticed the evidence of the pig in her shed when I edited the footage."

"Evie, come on. That's something only a true farmer like me could see." There was a long pause outside the door and then they both cracked up. When the laughter subsided, she added, "I assume you'll drive me downtown today?"

"It would be an honor," Evie said. "Although I fully expect the mayor to have security put me out."

Hannah cracked open the door. "Won't happen. Love me, love my videographer."

Evie caught her in a close-up, grinning as Hannah reared back. "I have an unexpected gift for this, don't I?"

Hannah slammed the door. "One day I'll thank you for it. When I have a full face of makeup and a nice blowout."

"Yes, ma'am. I mean, Miss Pemberton."

HANNAH SLAPPED the backside of the bronze German shepherd for luck before walking up the stairs to City Hall. She'd planned on running, for dramatic effect, but she was just too stiff, sore and bruised. Luckily none of that showed, at least according to Evie, because she wanted to put on a good front for Mayor Bradshaw.

Once upon a time just being a billionaire's daughter had been enough to impress him. Now she needed to do mental gymnastics to outwit him... or at least surround herself with people who could. Somehow, she'd become the face of the resistance for the old guard in Dog Town. From beleaguered farm novice to poster child in just two months. It had to be a record.

This time, the mayor was not only waiting in the reception area, he also opened the door for Hannah himself.

"See?" Evie hissed behind her. "Full retreat."

"Hannah, how nice of you to come," he said. "Evelyn, stand down with your camera or—"

"You'll throw me out on my butt," Evie finished.

"I'd never use that word, but I most certainly will ask you to leave," he said. "I'd rather you stay, really. You have a talent for handling difficult meetings."

Preceding him into his office, Hannah said, "There's no need for this to be difficult, Mayor. We both want the same thing."

His silvery eyebrows soared. "Really? I doubt that very much. Unless you came prepared to sell your land."

"Well, not that," Hannah said. "I assumed you wanted me to end my show. To stop talking about Dorset Hills. And that's what I want, too. It's time for me to start living my life instead of talking about it."

"How are you feeling today?" he asked, ushering her to one of two leather guest chairs. He'd turned them away from his desk to face each other. "You look well."

Instead of sitting behind his desk, he sat across from her, his knees almost touching her navy wool slacks that—as hard as she'd tried—were covered in pet hair. At a glance she could pick out Prima's, Leo's and even Beau's. There was even a small gray feather on her knee. It was a reminder to stay focused.

Evie stood near the door, hands at her side, letting Hannah run the show.

"I am well," she said. "It turns out getting attacked with a pitchfork gave me a new appreciation for farm life. Today I truly feel alive, sir."

His laugh sounded uneasy. "I'm pleased to hear it was... transformative. Life takes some surprising turns, doesn't it?"

"Indeed. Sir, I was very surprised when Sally told me she was feeding you personal information about me. I honestly never thought you'd care about my reproductive activity. I underestimated your curiosity."

He winced. "Perhaps we underestimated each other, Miss Pemberton."

"Let me say, I'm not at all surprised you'd use the information. Just that you'd run with it unconfirmed. Sally's hardly a reliable source."

"There are other ways," he began.

"No, there weren't. You sullied my reputation based on a rumor that just turned out to be true. My mother was right about you."

"Your mother? She's been gone for years. Don't tell me you and your—ahem, friends—are conducting seances now."

"My mom was very much alive when she spoke of you. You made quite an impression on her back when you and my dad ran in the same circles."

His shoulders straightened. "Really."

Hannah nodded. "She said people like you would come after people like us. I think she suspected I'd be back here one day, and that I'd be vulnerable to hometown land sharks."

"She didn't really know me," he said, leaning forward. "And you don't either, Hannah. I want to make this work... for both of us."

Shoving her chair away, she stared him down. "Just say whatever it is you want me to hear. Sir."

He leaned back in his chair and crossed his long legs elegantly at the knee. He was wearing grey socks with tiny Scottish terriers on them. It was a whimsical touch no doubt designed to put people at ease. It must work often enough, since he'd been elected in a landslide vote.

"I'd like you to cancel The Princess and the Pig," he said. "It's casting my town in a negative light, and I simply can't have that."

"On the contrary," she said. "I think it shows the capacity of your townspeople to come together for a worthy cause. It shows community at its best—and sometimes at its worst, I suppose. I mean, it's obviously not positive when a citizen goes after a neighbor with a pitchfork."

He closed his eyes for a second. "That story cannot air. People wouldn't feel safe here."

"Sally's in custody now," Hannah said. "We're well on the way to a happy ending."

"Let me repeat my request: Cancel. Your. Show."

She raised her eyebrows encouragingly. "And...? If I do...?"

"It should be enough that your mayor asks," he said. "But since you seem to need more, I offer to stop pressing you to sell your land."

"Meaning you promise to stop sabotaging me with silly policy changes and slander?"

He angled his chair slightly away. "The City will pretend Runaway Farm doesn't exist."

Now Hannah leaned forward. "But I want this farm to exist. I want to build on this land and create an experience that will support your vision for Dog Town."

"My vision doesn't include pigs, Hannah," he said. "Nor dancing camels, for that matter. My vision for Dog Town centers exclusively around dogs." His dark eyes rolled toward the ceiling. "I don't understand why people have so much trouble with that concept. It's simple, really."

"It is simple. On the surface," Hannah said. "But it's so one-dimensional. That's why the old guard, like Bob, get so entrenched. There's no reason your vision can't be more inclusive. Look how popular my show is. People all over the world are fascinated by Dorset Hills. Tourism has increased. Obviously."

He turned back and his eyes narrowed. "There was rioting last night. Your fans treated the missing camel like a scavenger hunt, overturning everything they could and storming municipal buildings. Dorset Hills is known for its quaint charm. You're making a mockery of all we hold dear."

Reaching into her large bag, she pulled out the mayor's framed portrait. "The plaque here says, 'Speak Truth to Power,' and I want to do that today. It's time you started seeing the opportunities in front of you."

Evie spoke after a long silence. "She's right, sir. You should listen."

He actually covered his ears, ruffling his perfect silver hair. "I'll make myself clear, Hannah: you will never get a permit to build in Dorset Hills. Your farm is safe, but I cannot allow you to expand, I'm afraid."

"Mayor, I—"

"Call me Bill," he said. "The title isn't necessary anymore."

"Pardon me?"

He leaned in so close she could smell minty mouthwash. "You don't live in Dorset Hills anymore. I've severed your land and Sally Taylor's and given it to Wolff County." He stood and gestured for the door. "I assume you'll take your requests to expand to their council."

"Wait... what?" She turned to Evie. "Can he just do that?"

Evie nodded. "Mayors in towns like this are pretty much free agents," she said, staring at the mayor with clear green eyes. "Clever move, sir. Shady, but clever. I like to think I'd have thought of it if I still worked in politics."

"You lost your edge with that concussion, I'm afraid." He smiled, to show those slightly yellowed canine teeth. "I can still back your service dog center, though. Once your faculties return fully."

Hannah set the mayor's portrait on his desk. "Sir. Dorset Hills is my hometown."

"It always will be," he said, nudging her chair to get her to rise. "But now you live in Wolff County. It's not a town per se, but it could be. It doesn't have the natural assets of Dorset Hills, but your show will bring infinite possibilities." He offered her the framed portrait again and she crossed her arms. "Of course, you're welcome to shop here whenever you like," he said, chuckling as he walked her to the door. "No passport required."

CHAPTER TWENTY-SEVEN

"It's for the best," Remi said, as they stood outside Alvina's pasture later. "Bill Bradshaw is like the Terminator. He never gives up. There's no way you'd be able to build any kind of resort here while he's at the helm."

"But I don't want to build in Wolff County. Dorset Hills is the big draw. Why would anyone come?"

"Oh, Hannah," Remi said. "I know it hurts to lose to Bill, but in time you'll see you really won. Everything will be easier, cheaper and faster working through Wolff County. They'll be grateful to have you. Imagine what municipal support will feel like."

"But Dog Town is home."

"We're your home." Remi gestured around at the group that had assembled. "Half of us don't live in Dorset Hills proper. And yet it's our town."

"I had to move out," Cori said. "The air quality suffered after this mayor took office."

Maisie and Nika agreed.

"Even I don't live in Dorset Hills," Kinney Butterfield said. "And I work for the City."

Hannah pressed her lips together. They'd all done so much for her that she didn't want to sound like an entitled diva. The only entitled female in her household was Prima, who perched in her arms now. Unlike Leo, Prima never lolled, never pandered. She was ready to bristle and lunge at a moment's notice. There was something comforting in that. Everyone should have a terrier shield against life's slings and arrows.

"It'll be much calmer now," Duff said. "You need that, Hannah. Your inn or whatever you build needs to be an oasis. That could never happen when you're under siege. I promise I'll help you with permits and Evie will help with publicity when you open for business."

"You need that to raise a family, too," Remi said. "Now the mayor won't show up randomly and terrify your child."

Hannah laughed. "You've got a point, Remi."

"Most important of all, you need calm for your animals," Cori said. "Deer are flight animals."

"Deer?" Hannah asked, and then, "Oh no you don't."

"It's just a couple," Cori said. "For a few weeks, while they recover."

"That's what you said about the goats, and they're still here. My farm isn't your dumpster, Cori."

"And my rescues are not garbage." Cori's orange flares landed on her hips.

"Of course not." Hannah glanced away. "I didn't mean that."

"I know," Cori said, letting her off the hook for once. "That's hormones talking."

"And you're just grumpy because you were wrong about Sally Taylor," Hannah said.

"I wasn't wrong. She just lost her mind and didn't tell me."

James joined them. "Can we drop the talk about my sister's hormones? It makes me squeamish."

"Wait till you have to change diapers, Uncle Jay," Cori said, smirking as she flew into the pen to join Alvina.

James was wincing as he pulled his sister aside. "I bought something today," he told her. "I wanted you to hear it first from me."

"What? A nice sports car? Another Tibetan terrier?"

"Land," he said. "Sullivan helped me find something worth developing down the road."

"Wait a second. You bought land in Dorset Hills and I got kicked out?"

"I bought land today *because* you got kicked out. Now I have a significant investment in Dorset Hills. If Bill Bradshaw wants to be a jerk again, he'll need to think long and hard about it first." He glanced at Remi, who'd sidled over to Hannah. "As Remi said, Bill's like the Terminator."

Remi offered Leo to James, and he accepted the beagle. That told Hannah more about her brother's state of mind than anything else. If he needed beagle therapy, he was more stressed than she'd ever witnessed before.

"Thank you, Jay," she said. "If this means you're sticking around, I'm thrilled."

"I've already asked Duff to find me a place," he said. "No offense, but this farm's a zoo."

He glanced toward Alvina, but Hannah suspected he was really checking out Kinney, who was helping Cori examine the alpaca's feet for glass from Sally Taylor's kitchen.

"Go talk to her," she said.

"Who? Alvina?" he said, startled. "Dancing is more our thing."

"I've got news for you, brother. Alvina prefers dancing with Nick. He's always introducing new moves."

James gave her a sly look. "Let me talk to her, while Nick practices his moves on you."

She was still shaking her head when Nick came over. "Your brother gave me his blessing," he said.

"For what?" Her voice sounded sharper than she intended, but she didn't like the idea of being handed off between the two men.

Nick just smiled. "To take you to your driver's test next week. I'll borrow Evie's car."

"Bring the truck." She started walking along the fence, and he followed. "If it goes well, I'll drive you home in it."

"You're taking the test with a stick?" he asked.

"Someone once told me that anyone who really likes driving needs a standard transmission. I took him at his word."

"You're going to need a lot of practice this weekend," he said.

"No cameras," she said, staring over at Evie. She smiled at Hannah, clearly giving her blessing, too.

Nick ran his hand along the top rung of the fence and then said, "Ow."

"Welcome to life on a farm," she said, grinning. "The serenity comes with splinters."

"Sounds like a typical family to me," he said. "I like it."

He leaned over, and the way he looked at her raised goosebumps on her arms. Was he going to kiss her? Right here in front of everyone?

Closer... closer... their lips barely touched when a sudden movement caught her eye and she jumped. But it was just Alvina.

"Hold that thought," Nick said, grinning as he pulled away.

Alvina's big sweet eyes were fixed on Nick, and he knew what to do. Flapping his arms, he took off, racing along outside the fence with the alpaca frolicking inside. He managed to croon her favorite song as he ran.

Laughing at their antics, Hannah clutched the terrier tighter, till she squirmed. "Never mind, Prima," she said. "We're pack now. No matter how much you fight, I'm never letting you go. And no matter what side of the county line we're on... we're home."

So... what's next in Dog Town? Kinney Butterfield has been working hard to bring down the mayor's flawed regime from the inside. But will this dedicated dog cop lose her sharp edge when a heartbroken dog and a distracting man come into her life? Either way, fireworks are guaranteed in Dorset Hills for Independence Day—and not just for Hannah and Nick . Follow along in *Bold and Blue in Dog Town*

Please sign up for my author newsletter at **Sandyrideout.com** to receive the FREE prequel, *Ready or Not in Dog Town*, as well as *A Dog with Two Tales*, the prequel to the Bought-the-Farm series. You'll also get the latest news and far too many pet photos.

Before you move on to the next book, if you would be so

kind as to leave a review of this one, that would be great. I appreciate the feedback and support. Reviews stoke the fires of my creativity!

Other Books by Sandy Rideout and Ellen Riggs

Dog Town Series:

- *Ready or Not in Dog Town* (The Beginning)
- *Bitter and Sweet in Dog Town* (Labor Day)
- *A Match Made in Dog Town* (Thanksgiving)
- *Lost and Found in Dog Town* (Christmas)
- *Calm and Bright in Dog Town* (Christmas)
- *Tried and True in Dog Town* (New Year's)
- *Yours and Mine in Dog Town* (Valentine's Day)
- *Nine Lives in Dog Town* (Easter)
- *Great and Small in Dog Town* (Memorial Day)
- *Bold and Blue in Dog Town* (Independence Day)
- *Better or Worse in Dog Town* (Labor Day)

Boxed Sets:

- *Mischief in Dog Town - Books 1-3*
- *Mischief in Dog Town - Books 4-7*
- *Mischief in Dog Town - Books 8-10*

Bought-the-Farm Cozy Mystery Series

- *A Dog with Two Tales (prequel)*
- *Dogcatcher in the Rye*
- *Dark Side of the Moo*
- *A Streak of Bad Cluck*
- *Till the Cat Lady Sings*
- *Alpaca Lies*
- *Twas the Bite Before Christmas*
- *Swine and Punishment*
- *Don't Rock the Goat*
- *Swan with the Wind*

Made in the USA
Monee, IL
04 September 2021

77313979R00128